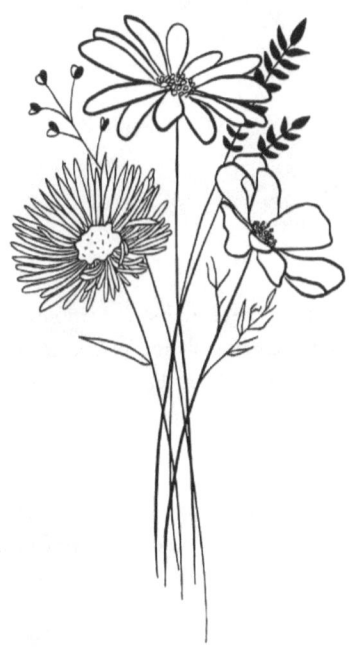

Original Book Cover & Character Art by @GloInkDesigns, Athira Jayachandran.

Discreet Book Cover Art by @LemonLee.Shop, Megan Lee.

Editing by Sam Stringert, @samspeededits.

1st edition 2026.

Flower People

Brews, Blooms, and Books #2

Ashley Claire

For everyone who's gone through the unimaginable.
You are worthy of another love story.

Content Warnings

Oh Hi!

As always, thanks for buying my book!

This book is full of love, romance, and . . . well . . . *smut*

I know *GASP*

Similarly to Coffee People, if this book will cause you to not be able to make eye contact with me, please stop reading now.

If you'd like to still think of me as adorably innocent, turn back now.

Thanksgiving potatoes are still more important.

Thanks, and love you bunches! <3

XOXO, Ashley

Real Content Warnings:

- Grief

- Depression

- Explicit Language

- Death of a Parent

- Death of a Spouse

- Explicit Sexual Content

- Alcohol use

- Mental Health Representation

Flower People Playlist

✦ **Cruel Summer**
Taylor Swift

✦ **Shape of You**
Ed Sheeran

✦ **Pink Pony Club**
Chappel Roan

✦ **I love you, I'm sorry**
Gracie Abrams

✦ **You're Gonna Go Far**
Noah Kahan

✦ **God damn you're beautiful**
Chester See

✦ **Can't Help Falling in Love**
Kina Grannis

✦ **Fast**
Demi Lovato

✦ **Beautiful Things**
Benson Boone

✦ **Free**
KPop Demon Hunters

✦ **King of my Heart**
Taylor Swift

✦ **My Man on his Willpower**
Sabrina Carpenter

✦ **Flowers**
Miley Cyrus

✦ **Daisies**
Justin Bieber

✦ **Lost in the Woods**
Jonathan Groff

✦ **Roses (ft. ROZES)**
The Chainsmokers

✦ **Carry You Home**
Alex Warren

✦ **Surrender**
Natalie Taylor

✦ **When I fall in Love**
Celine Dion (ft. Clive Griffin)

✦ **In Other Words**
Ed Sheeran

What did the flower say after it told a joke?
joke?
I was just pollen your leg!

Chapter One

Jess

I FUCKED UP.

I showed up for my first day of work at my dream job. I was looking like a million bucks, and feeling like a trillion—and the owner was *him*.

The guy who shoved me out of his home the morning before, telling me I needed to leave after spending a magical night together.

I didn't care at that moment yesterday morning. I figured I'd never see the asshole again, but now he is my *boss*. He's seen me naked; he's done absolutely mind-blowing things with my body. I've had more orgasms with the man standing in front of me than my most recent ex-boyfriend of four months.

The night we spent together felt like something. I'm so naive. I'm probably too young for him, or just too stupid. I have to be an idiot to think we had some kind of magical connection. I was a giddy little school girl, and he said I needed to leave.

I can barely look him in the eyes, and yet, I have to work for him.

48 hours earlier...

I've finally fucking made it.

I honestly thought I'd die alone in the small town of Daisy Ridge, but I somehow got my dream job. I'm going to be a lead florist at the cutest flower shop in Rose Point. Blossom Bliss Corner is the most gorgeous flower shop I've ever seen. It's a little maroon storefront, tightly wedged in between the city buildings. The name is written in script across the top of the building. They have buckets and buckets of flowers tiered out front—their captivating colors drawing you in. Inside there is every style of floral arrangement you could ever imagine.

I did several interviews with them over the phone. Eventually, I went in and did a few arrangements for the current lead florist, Becky, who absolutely loved me! I mean, how could she not?

Unfortunately, the owner's daughter was home sick the day I came in to do my arrangements, so he let Becky make the call. She said it was a no-brainer, I had to be the new florist. I felt slightly weird about taking a job in such a small place without meeting the owner, but I was sure he would be awesome. With a flower shop like that, how could he not be?

I moved into my new apartment on Stem Street, and my best friend Lindsey and I are going out to celebrate tonight. Lindsey owns the cutest bookstore in Rose Point. Someday I hope I can own my own flower shop, but for now, I'm just happy to be here in the city.

Don't get me wrong, I know I'll miss Daisy Ridge. I will miss my big sister and dad like crazy, but I'm excited to spend more time with my fun friends in the city. I was just destined for city life; the small town vibes never really fit me.

Tonight, I'm ready to party it up with my bestie! We are going to Bloomsy Bar for our first few drinks, and then going over to Stem Street Station, that way I'm nice and close to home. I'm planning on getting crazy tonight. I haven't spent a night in the city in a *long* time, and Lindsey and I are going to have the freaking best time now that I *live* here. I seriously can't wait to spend every day with her.

It still feels surreal.

I'm still unpacking my new apartment, so there are boxes all over my tiny new studio. It's so small compared to the two bedroom I was renting in Daisy Ridge. I'm probably going to have to downsize because right now the boxes are stacked in every direction higher than my head. It's a problem for a later Jess though, because right now I'm focused on going out.

There is a knock at the door, and I swing it open, screeching loudly as I do. "AHHHHHH!" Lindsey shouts while jumping up and down on the other side.

"You're here! You have a place! We doin' the damn thing! We are making dreams come true, bitch!" she shouts excitedly.

My next-door neighbor Phyllis, who I had the *joy* of meeting earlier, swings open her door. Lindsey turns to look at her. Phyllis sticks her head out, glares at Lindsey and I, and then yells "Will you broads keep it down? I can't hear my damn television. I need to hear my *Sixty Minutes*!" and then slams her door shut again.

Lindsey turns back around to face me, whispering "Oops, sorry," as her face twists into a grimace. She and I start laughing quietly as I usher her into my studio and close the door behind her.

"Sweet neighbor you got there!" She moves her thumb back over her shoulder gesturing to where Phyllis lives. She looks around my new place, hands on her hips, before muttering, "I mean this in the nicest way, but this place is kind of a pit. Do you want me to help you unpack tonight instead of going out?"

"Hell no!" I shout at her. "It's my first night living in the same city as my best friend! We are going out to party and celebrate!"

"Okay, okay, I just know you start your new job in a couple days. It might be nice to not be cramped with boxes by then . . ." She gestures around to the array of boxes stacked high everywhere.

"Ugh, it's fine, Linds. I'll unpack tomorrow. Let's goooooo!" I pump my fist in the air and she laughs.

"All right, let's get ready!" She turns toward my bathroom, carefully moving around all the boxes. It's an utter maze to get there but we make it into my cramped bathroom, and she starts laughing.

"What's so funny?" I glare at her.

"Oh nothing, it's just that this bathroom is not big enough for both of us to do makeup in." She giggles. "Got another mirror somewhere? I can just sit on some boxes, make a little vanity out of them?"

"You're being a bitch . . ." I mumble, pulling a mirror out from a drawer. It's luckily the only bathroom drawer I already unpacked. I'm grateful I did, otherwise Lindsey would probably make another comment about how we shouldn't go out tonight.

"Do you have a speaker unpacked yet? I can put on some music?" She pulls her phone out of her jeans pocket.

"Yeah, it's on the counter," I say, gesturing to where my tiny counter is. The counter isn't even big enough for two barstools, but I squeezed two in there anyway.

Lindsey starts playing her 'going out' playlist, which takes off with "Cruel Summer" by Taylor Swift, because we are Eras Tour girlies.

I plug in the curling iron so I can start curling my long, dark brown hair. I think my hair is my best feature. It holds curls so well, and I love to style it like old-school Hollywood. I typically use Sabrina Carpenter pictures as my inspiration. Her hair is so damn gorgeous.

While the curling iron heats up, I start cleaning off the makeup I'm currently wearing, so I can do a fresh style for tonight. You'll never see me without makeup on. I would be embarrassed as hell if someone saw me without makeup. My fair skin and bright blue eyes just don't have the same impact without makeup and my self-tanner.

Once I have my hair and makeup done, I rummage through a box with my heels in it. I'm only 5' on a good day, which makes me the shortest of all my family and friends, so I usually always wear heels to make my legs appear longer.

I find the sparkly black heels I was looking for, and make my way back through the maze of boxes to set them on the counter.

I look over at Lindsey, who did in fact create a little vanity out of boxes. She looks adorable. Lindsey doesn't do as much with her hair and makeup as I do, but she doesn't need it. She is naturally gorgeous. Her long red hair cascades down in perfect beach waves. Her cheeks are lightly freckled highlighting her little blue eyes. She's wearing a gorgeous red crochet crop top that has a maroon bralette underneath, and her high-waisted jean shorts hug her curves perfectly.

She looks over at me while applying her lip gloss. "What are you going to wear tonight?"

I look down at the robe I'm currently wearing. "I don't know. I don't have everything unpacked yet . . . I'll definitely wear my signature black leather jacket."

"Well, duh!" She laughs. "You practically can't go anywhere without it."

I walk over to an open box of clothes on the floor, and start rummaging through it. "Is a dress too much? What are the vibes we are going for tonight?" I say into the box.

"I mean . . . I'm wearing this." I turn and Lindsey gestures to her current outfit.

"Ugh, okay, I mean, I'll probably wear a dress anyway," I grunt. I don't really feel confident in anything else lately.

"You do you boo!" Lindsey smiles.

I pull out one of my favorite red dresses. It's a tight fitted red dress with halter straps that criss-cross at the neck.

Once I'm dressed, I fluff up my hair, running my fingers through it one last time. I touch up my makeup and apply my signature red lipstick.

I head out of the bathroom where Lindsey is waiting for me while texting on her phone.

"You ready to get crazy?" I ask her.

"Oh I was born ready!" she says, and we laugh as we link our arms together and make our way out.

I'm planning on finding the hottest guy in this city tonight and making him mine.

Chapter Two

JULIAN

I glance at the clock.

I have twenty more minutes. Only twenty minutes before I take a giant leap that I don't think I'm ready to take.

I stand in front of the mirror fumbling with the buttons on my shirt. It's been five years since I've gone out. Five years since I've left my adorable kiddo with a babysitter and taken time for myself. It's been five years since Hannah died.

Tonight isn't a date, not exactly, it's just drinks. Just friends, and just ... an invitation to go out and "see who's out there." My buddy, David, had said it casually over coffee last week, like it was the most normal thing in the world. *"You gotta get back out there, man. Come out with us*

Friday. No pressure. It's just beer, some music, and maybe you'll meet someone. Just come feel human again."

Hannah's photo still sits on my dresser, just like it always has. She's smiling, frozen in time. For years, I couldn't picture ever sitting across from another woman, couldn't imagine laughter that didn't sound like hers.

Hannah was my best friend. It wasn't a passionate relationship, but it was comfortable. I never really dated, so I don't even know where to start now.

Everyone is right though, I need to feel human again. I need to start moving in a new direction. If not for me, for Jules, the real love of my life . . . my six-year-old daughter.

A wave of guilt creeps in. I reach out, almost involuntarily, touching the edge of Hannah's photo. "I don't know if I'm doing the right thing," I whisper. "But I think . . . I think I need to try."

I pick the photo up, and slide it into a nearby drawer. Guilt nags at me.

The guys are convinced that since it's been five years, I need to get laid. I'm not so convinced, but on the off chance I do, I can't have this smiling picture of Hannah watching me.

There are a few tears behind my eyes, but they don't fall. I take a deep breath.

This isn't about replacing Hannah. No one ever could. It's about finding space in my heart to feel something again. Maybe not love, not yet at least—but something. Maybe just laughter, or hope. I've been so closed off to my emotions for such a long time, and I want to be the best man that I can be for my little girl.

The guilt is sharper than I expected. This is the first time in five years I'm going out. Not just *out*, but *out-out*. I'm not going to a family barbecue, or the grocery store. I'm not going to the cemetery, and this isn't another polite conversation where people look at me with eyes full of sympathy. This is real life again. This is going to be loud bars, strangers, and laughter that isn't softened by loss.

But being the best I can be means I should put myself out there. Or at least rekindle some of these friendships I've ignored. That's the whole reason I agreed to go in the first place: for my friends, for people like David. People who have been there for me the last five years who deserve a real friendship in return.

My mom took Jules for a sleepover. It's Jules' first time sleeping over anywhere. She was *so* excited, and so was my mom. I shouldn't be worried, but a small part of me is. What if something happens while I'm out drinking? I take a deep breath, and calm my nerves. Jules is great, probably doing better with my mom than she does with me, honestly. She and my mom are probably doing all the girly things that Jules wants so desperately.

The headlights of David's car flash through the window. It's time.

I grab my wallet and keys, and take one last look at the house, the house I lived in with Hannah, and step outside.

The sky is turning pink at the edges. The evening air is cool and holds the promise of something unknown.

What will I even talk about? Do I still know how to flirt, or did I leave that in my youth?

It hits me then: I'm not ready for this. My stomach is in knots, and the nerves threaten to send me back inside and into the bathroom. My hands are shaky, and my heart is heavy, but my feet are still moving.

And that is something. It's more than I've done before.

I don't know what tonight will bring. Maybe it will be awkward. Maybe it will be a disaster. Or maybe it will be a small beginning, a step in the right direction.

And that maybe is enough.

We enter Stem Street Station late. I'm tired, but I'm enjoying myself. We've already gone to a couple other bars and I'm feeling good. I've loosened up. I'm not meeting any girls tonight, but I'm having fun with a few guys I've missed hanging out with.

As we enter Stem Street, the bell above the door gives a short jingle as I step into the bar. It isn't loud; it's more like a sigh than a welcome. The air inside is thicker than I remember. It's heavy with old wood, spilled whiskey, and the hum of half-hearted conversation. This place hasn't changed much the past five years. That is either comforting or tragic, I'm not sure which.

David and Michael laugh at some joke they just heard outside. David slaps my back and nudges me to make our way over to the bar.

My shoes make soft thuds against the floor as I cross over to the bar behind them. The same scratches decorate the mahogany wood floor. There is still the same crooked leg on the third stool. I hesitate for a second, because this was always Hannah's seat when we came together. I sigh, and then sit down anyway.

The bartender has a new face. He's younger, with a tattoo of an owl on his forearm and eyes that look like they've seen too much, too soon.

"What'll it be?" the bartender asks me, polite but distracted.

"Jameson. Neat," I answer.

The drink comes fast. I stare at it for a long second before taking a sip.

The burn is immediate and welcome. It settles low, beneath my ribs, like a reminder that some things still work the way they used to.

That's when I see her.

She is sitting at the far end of the bar, framed by the soft golden glow of a hanging light. Her hair is a mess of chocolate waves, as she laughs at something the guy next to her just said, but it isn't a polite laugh. It's a real, unguarded, carefree laugh.

It's the kind of laugh people write songs about. The kind of laugh that makes a woman beautiful. Because she isn't trying to be beautiful, she just *is*.

I look down at my drink. Five years. It's been five years of keeping my head down, working, disappearing into myself. I didn't come here looking for anything. I just wanted to remember what it felt like to be *in* a place instead of *outside* of one.

But now I'm watching her, a perfect stranger, the way a man watches a fire from across the room. Drawn to it, wary of it, and wondering if it will burn me or keep me warm.

I turn back to my glass, and take another sip. This isn't the kind of story where I just walk over and say something clever.

Maybe I will say hello.

Maybe not.

But the drink is warm in my chest, and for the first time in a long time, the night feels less like a weight and more like a door.

David nudges me. "Earth to Julian," he chuckles. "Did we lose you there for a second?"

I turn to look at him. "Ha, yeah, sorry man."

"No worries, it's the chair isn't it?" He rubs my shoulder. "I'm happy you came out tonight. Hannah would want this, man."

"Yeah, you're right. Thanks, man." I sigh. I immediately feel guilty for looking at this woman across the room.

And even though I feel immense guilt, my eyes immediately move back to find her again. I couldn't even stop myself if I tried. She's doing a shot with two girlfriends now. The guy who had her laughing before looks defeated next to her.

David must notice me staring, because he leans over and says, "Go say hi. Buy her a drink."

I look over at him, and he winks.

"Oh no, I don't think I can," I tell him.

"Sure you can." He puts his hand up, gesturing to the bartender.

The bartender comes over. "What's up David? What can I get ya?"

"Two shots of Jameson for my buddy here," he says, slapping my shoulder, "and a shot of tequila for me please."

Chapter Three

JESS

My mission for the night was to find a hot guy and immediately take him home, but the evening took a turn once we arrived at Bloomsy Bar.

We walked in to meet our friend, Brooke, and she held up her brand-new engagement ring screaming, and so the evening immediately shifted to a girl's night out. My sole focus now is getting our bestie drunk and sending her home to her new fiancé to celebrate. We are celebrating her, and it would be selfish of me to focus on finding a man now.

After spending some time at Bloomsy Bar, we make our way over to Stem Street Station.

We take shots, have drinks, and I'm feeling really light and fun by the time Brooke heads home to her new fiancé.

"Gosh, I'm so happy for her." Lindsey sighs. "I hope I find that happiness someday," she says wistfully, as we wave goodbye to Brooke.

Lindsey is a romantic in the worst way. She's pretty introverted and quiet, and I'm the loud one who drags her out of the house. She probably would have much preferred to stay back and unpack my apartment tonight, honestly.

Although she's gorgeous, I worry she won't find the epic love she's looking for because she doesn't put herself out there enough. Even tonight, men come up to us at the bar, and she brushes them off. I know if she tried, she'd have every single man in this town vying for her attention.

Yet, she is focused on her bookstore, and I don't blame her. My sister, Sarah, was the same way about her coffee shop until a few months ago.

Anyway, now that Brooke has gone home to her fiancé, it's just Lindsey and me. I look around Stem Street Station, and there are groups of men and women everywhere. I glance across the bar and see a group of three guys taking shots and laughing.

The one closest to us is fine as hell. He's tall, with dark blond hair and gorgeous blue eyes. He probably gets a lot of ladies around here.

Lindsey taps me on the shoulder. "I think I'm almost done here too, Jess. I have to get up early and I'm tired."

Lindsey doesn't drink, not for any reason other than she says she just doesn't like it. Sometimes I wonder if there is more to it than that, but she's my best friend. She would tell me if there was something to tell.

I smile at her. "Just give me five minutes? There is a guy I'm dying to talk to on the other side of the bar. His two friends look cute too." I wiggle my eyebrows at her.

She sighs. "You have five minutes Jess, and then I'm out."

"You're the best friend, you know that?" I grin at her, and grab her hand, pulling her to the other side of the bar.

"Yeah, I do know that." She groans as I drag her across the room.

I walk up to the man I was eyeing. "Hi!" I say to him.

He immediately locks eyes with me. "Uh, hey," he nearly whispers.

I giggle, mostly because I'm drunk, but also because his nervousness is so cute.

His friend slaps his back. "This is my buddy, Julian. I'm David," he points to the guy on the other side of him, "and this is Michael."

I smile. "I'm Jess, this is my best friend, Lindsey. She owns Rose Point Books. Have you guys heard of it?"

The guy named Michael nods. "Yeah, I thought you looked familiar!" he says happily. "I love your store."

Lindsey smiles. "Thank you, it was my grandmother's."

I interrupt, "But Lindsey has made a lot of changes. She has made the place what it is today!" I grin, as Lindsey swats at my shoulder. I'm proud of her, even if she won't be proud of herself. She's put so much work into that store, and still just brushes it off like it was passed down.

David shoots me a sly grin as I finish hyping up Lindsey. "Would you guys like a drink?" he asks.

"I'd love to do a shot, maybe with this guy." I gesture to Julian, and caress his shoulder. His gorgeous blue eyes draw me in like a moth to a flame.

He looks like trouble, and I'm all for it.

"Oh I don't know," he mumbles, "we just did a few . . ."

"All the more reason to just give in, and do one more with a pretty girl." I boop his nose.

He looks flustered by the touch, but I think he secretly loved it.

"Uh okay, just one though . . ." He smiles politely.

It's adorable. I want to kiss him silly. I mean, I wanted to kiss his gorgeous lips even before he smiled. Maybe I'm more intoxicated than I thought I was.

All of us, even Lindsey with her Dr. Pepper, hold our glasses up to cheers.

"What are we toasting to?" Julian asks.

I smile at him. "New beginnings." I'm so excited for my new life in the city. I have a feeling this is the start of my best chapter yet.

He smiles, more genuine this time. "I love the sound of that."

I tip my shot back and swallow before mumbling, "I love the sound of *you*."

I wake up in an unknown bed. Crap, I lost track of the shots.

I've only lost track of the number of drinks I had one other time, and if my sister Sarah were here, she'd kill me.

I groan, and sit up. My head pounds. It feels like my body and brain are punishing me for all the fun I had last night.

I try to pry my eyes open, but the violent sunlight poking through the blinds threatens to bring me to tears. My head throbs like someone has lodged a jackhammer behind my eyes. I lay back and squint at the ceiling, but it is spinning slightly, just enough to make my stomach roll.

I try to sit up, but it's a mistake. The world lurches sideways, and my stomach gives a threatening twist. I collapse back onto the bed, groaning. My phone buzzes somewhere in the room, but it sounds like it is doing it from inside a jet engine.

Fragments of the night before drift back in pieces. There was laughter, hands, lips, tongues, and good god it was magical. If I remember correctly it was one of the most amazing orgasmic experiences of my life.

One orgasm seems to just play on repeat in my head. I was on all fours, and he did this magical thing with his hand while he thrusted so hard into me from behind, I saw stars. As soon as he twisted my hair around his hand and aggressively bit my shoulder, I was done.

The image in my head has me hot and bothered just lying here in his bed. I grin as I roll over, but he isn't next to me.

While the orgasms were nice, he was also kind and funny. He was the kind of guy I've always imagined I'd end up with. We had a lot in common, from the few conversations I can piece together.

I hope he is as hot as I remember from my drunken state.

I look around the room; it's cozy. Neutrals, mixed with some sage greens, because we are millennials after all. There are lots of pillows and blankets, and a beautiful oak armoire. I get the feeling I didn't examine it at all last night, because it looks like it has had a woman's touch at some point. I pray he's not married.

I would be sick to my stomach if I was a homewrecker here.

I force myself up out of the bed.

It's time to face the music.

There is a bathroom off the bedroom. I head in to try to make myself sexy and presentable. It's a hard task but I think I do a pretty good job.

I even use my finger as a toothbrush and give my teeth a little scrub with his toothpaste.

When I finally look decent, I make my way out of the bathroom, and exit the cozy bedroom.

I move down a hallway, to an open concept kitchen, a shared space with a dining table and living room.

It's all decorated beautifully. There is a large gray couch that looks plush and so comfortable. My pounding head immediately makes me want to go sit on it and fall back asleep. I force myself to stay upright though, because Julian is in the kitchen. His back is currently to me as he drinks a cup of coffee. I clear my throat to let him know I'm there.

He turns around, and even hungover with bed head, the man is gorgeous. I did good. I internally pat myself on the back, because I'm damn proud of this one.

Yep, I could *definitely* see this man being a long-term thing.

I smile. "Hey," I whisper.

"Hey," he whispers back.

Tension fills the air like a thick blanket.

"So . . ." I sigh. "Want some breakfast?" I ask, hopeful.

"Oh, uhm, no," he mumbles, crossing his arms across his chest. "Actually I need you to leave."

"I'm sorry?" I snap. Is this man kicking me to the curb already? I just walked out here; what if I was still sleeping?

"Sorry, yeah, I . . . uh . . . need you to go, quickly actually," he says, louder this time, while shifting on his feet.

I'm taken aback. He isn't telling me he has plans or that he needs to get to work, he's literally just telling me to leave.

I'm hurt and angry at this point.

"Are you . . . serious right now?" I ask angrily.

"Yeah, sorry." He picks up his phone, and starts typing on it, completely ignoring me.

Maybe it's my own insecurities that are fueling my anger, or maybe I actually have every right to be mad.

I feel so damn stupid. I know we were both drunk, but I felt sparks. I felt butterflies in my stomach. I felt all the feelings everyone in the movies tells me I should feel when I meet someone special. I don't know where I thought this was going, but I definitely didn't think after the moments I remember from last night, he would immediately kick me out.

"I'm sorry, I thought . . . Are you married or something? Am I a homewrecker? I knew this house was too nice for a single guy!" I start shouting. I can't help it. I feel insane right now, and my head still throbs.

"No, I uh . . . I'm . . . I just need you to leave," he says.

"Oh my god, fine!" I throw my hands up and shout, "I'm so damn stupid. I thought . . . I thought we had fun, I thought this was different." I grab my shoes and purse, and storm out of the house before I can hear another word from him.

I'm so upset with myself. I can't believe I fell for this.

I'll find someone better than him. I'm never seeing that stupid man ever again.

Chapter Four

JULIAN

I SCREWED UP.

I could've just told her the truth. I should've told her my six-year-old daughter was going to be home any second, and I needed her to get the hell out before she saw her.

I didn't though. I just told her to leave.

Honestly, I got scared. I felt a lot of feelings, really fast. I didn't *want* feelings last night, I wanted to get out of the house, and maybe see what was out there.

Not bring someone home with me, and definitely not to *feel* something.

But I couldn't help it. Jess was intoxicating. She was sexy, smart, and funny. She was confident and bold. She was everything I wish I could be again. I know it's in me somewhere. It's just been buried for five years in a heap of grief.

When we had a couple deep conversations last night, I realized I could see this. I could see myself dating her, and I freaked out. So I told her she needed to leave, and left it at that.

I'm not ready for anything. The only reason I let loose and was ready for sex was because I was drinking.

In the sober light of day, I wasn't ready. The guilt is eating me alive.

I think the thing that eats at me the most after all these years is that Hannah and I weren't great together. We didn't have a passionate, loving relationship. We were best friends who started hooking up and got pregnant. We got married because we loved each other as friends, and that was enough for us at the time.

But a few months after Jules was born, she said she wanted more. She wanted romance and passion, and I told her I didn't think I had it in me.

I keep replaying the same scene in my mind. Where her hands reached for something I never quite knew how to give. That real passion. The kind that comes naturally to some people, like breathing or laughter. But for me, it was always something I had to *try* for, something I had to shape and imitate, hoping she wouldn't notice the seams.

And now she's gone.

It's strange how grief can echo with all the things we didn't do, rather than the things we did. I loved her, I know I did but she wanted a fire I never lit. She wanted to be consumed, and I gave her warmth instead. I thought warmth was enough. I thought ... we had time.

But passion was the language she dreamed of, and I never learned to speak it fluently.

So now I sit here with this ache. A guilt that keeps turning over like a stone in my chest. People keep telling me none of this is my fault, that love has many shapes, that she knew I cared. But they didn't see the way her eyes dimmed sometimes, like she was trying to convince herself that what we had was what she needed. They didn't hear the quiet way she asked, "Do you ever feel like you need ... more?"

And I didn't know how to answer.

I wonder if that makes me unworthy now. Unworthy of passion, unworthy of fire, unworthy of the kind of love she craved. Part of me feels like wanting it now, after losing her ... it's a betrayal. Like I only learned the value of flame by standing in the ashes.

Maybe this is the punishment, to finally understand the ache she carried.

To want what I couldn't give her.

And to believe, deep down, that I don't deserve to want it at all.

I went to therapy briefly after she passed. My therapist told me that as my best friend, Hannah would want me to find my romance. She'd want me to find that person, for me, and for our daughter.

So I stopped going to therapy, because she's wrong. I don't deserve to have the one thing Hannah always longed for.

Eventually I quit my job, and took over Hannah's business . . . in flowers.

Hannah opened a small flower shop here in Rose Point one year before Jules was born. When she passed away, it became my responsibility.

So now, I'm a single dad who is trying to run a flower shop, and make it successful enough that my little girl and I can survive.

The real kicker is, I don't know shit about flowers.

Luckily, Hannah left some awesome employees behind. She prepared them well, and they've been great.

I glance at my watch. Where the hell is my mom?

Just as I'm about to call her and see where she is, the front door swings open.

"DAD!" Jules shouts, throwing her bag on the ground and running over to me, arms wide.

"Jujubee!" I shout, throwing my own arms out wide.

She tackles me in a bear hug. "Oh, kiddo. I missed you." I squeeze her tight, and kiss the side of her head.

"I know. I told Nana you would." She releases me, and boops my nose.

That one little movement reminds me so much of when Jess did it last night that I'm momentarily thrown off. I shake my head to get back into the present moment.

I force a laugh. "You're one of a kind, kid. How was your sleepover?"

"It was amazing! We watched The *Gabby's Dollhouse* movie, ate popcorn, and look! Nana did my nails, aren't they pretty, Dad?" She holds her hands up for my inspection. Each nail is a different color.

"Wow, they are gorgeous Jujubee! I love them." I smile at her and squeeze her hands.

My mom interrupts us. "And how was your night, Dad?" she questions.

It's like she has that motherly intuition telling her something is wrong. Like she knows I've been bad.

"It was nice. Good to get out, but I'm good for a while now. I'm happy at home with my Jujubee!" I smile at Jules, and give her little hand a squeeze. She giggles, and runs down the hall.

"I'm going to go say hi to my stuffies!" she shouts as she runs.

I smile watching her run down the hall. The kid is everything to me. I hate leaving her. Even if logically I know time with her nana is important too.

I turn back to my mom. She stands with her arms crossed in front of her. Like she's waiting for me to say more about last night. Jokes on her, though, I'm not saying anything. I'm a steel vault.

We stand there, both waiting for the other person to break. Finally, after a minute, my mom sighs, and walks over and wraps her arms around me in a hug.

"I just want you to be happy again," she whispers.

My eyes threaten to water. I want to be happy again, too. I'm just not sure I know how anymore. I'm in a vicious cycle of self-sabotage.

When she releases me, I tell her, "Thanks again, Mom. Was she okay last night?"

"She was more than okay, Julian! She needed this as much as you did. She needed some girl time. We had a blast." Mom gives my shoulder a squeeze before heading down the hall after Jules.

I know we all needed this. My dad passed away about ten years ago, and I know my mom has been lonely lately. She doesn't get to spend as much time with her granddaughter as she used to since Jules started kindergarten this past school year.

I sigh. My mom can come hangout with Jules whenever. I'm going to keep doing what I'm doing and plan on never having to see Jess ever again.

Chapter Five

JESS

"I SERIOUSLY CANNOT BELIEVE that jackass kicked me out!" I shout into the phone at Lindsey.

I'm trying to unlock my apartment door, but fumbling with the keys.

"Babe, you met him at a bar and went home with him after knowing him, what five minutes? What did you expect?" Lindsey sighs.

I mean she's right, but she's supposed to be on my side.

"Lindsey, be Team Jess please," I grunt, while finally getting my key in the door.

Phyllis sticks her head out. "Ugh, what a horrible walk of shame you are doing! Where is your class?"

"Up your ass along with that stick, Phyllis!" I shout at her while moving into the door and slamming it behind me.

I look around. I need to unpack and get semi-organized before I start my new job in the morning.

Realizing I'm still on the phone with Lindsey, I ask, "What time are you done working today? Want to come over and help me unpack?"

She sighs, and then chuckles. "You know, I offered to do that last night."

"Yeah, yeah, but what about tonight?" I beg.

"Of course I will come help you tonight, but do not expect me to be with you every night for the rest of your existence. I like being alone and reading sometimes, you know?" She giggles.

"Yes ma'am! See you around six? Do you want Chinese?" I ask.

"Nah, how about pizza and soda? Cause we are classy ladies," she says with a laugh.

"You got it, see ya tonight. I'll try and get a lot done before then." I giggle.

I hang up with Lindsey and look around at the mess of boxes. It feels daunting and I'm not ready. I decide to procrastinate for a few more minutes by calling my big sister, Sarah.

I haven't told her about my new city life yet.

I call Sarah, and she answers on the first ring. "Helloooooo," she sings.

"Hi babe, how's Daisy Ridge? Give me the tea, what have I missed?" I quiz.

Sarah laughs. "You've been gone for like two days and this is Daisy Ridge, you haven't missed anything other than Carol finally made a personal TikTok account . . ."

I burst into laughter. Carol is an older woman who works at my sister's coffee shop. She's also Sarah's self-proclaimed "bestie for the restie."

Sarah recently had some travel bloggers in her coffee shop to help with business, and one particular video of Carol winking and singing Mariah Carey while brewing up coffee has gone viral.

Since the event, Carol has been wearing an "As Seen On TV" button during her shifts and talking about "Tik-Tacs."

"No she did not!" I chuckle.

"She did. If you want to follow her, her username is wildgingerbarista," she deadpans.

I literally cannot stop laughing, because that is entirely too accurate. There is a sudden banging on my wall followed by Phyllis yelling, "Will you keep it down in there? I can't hear my show!"

I sigh.

"My neighbor is a real bitch. She could use some Carol charm," I mutter.

"I heard that you dumb broad!" she yells again.

"Remind me to look up soundproofing," I whisper to Sarah.

She laughs. "Oh boy, it's only been a couple days and I already miss you."

"I miss you too, sis," I say quietly, like it's some kind of secret. "So, I have some bad news. I know I said I was going to come home for our weekly family dinners, but I don't think I should for a couple months. I'm not sure what my work schedule will be, and I think I need to adjust and get settled before I start trying to come home all the time."

Sarah pauses briefly before saying, "It's okay, Jess. Take all the time you need to settle. We are proud of you. Dad and I will be okay, we will miss you, but we will be okay. Just don't forget to call and check in with him too."

"I won't. I'll call him," I mumble, feeling like a child being lectured. Of course I was going to tell my dad.

Sarah sighs. "Anyways, how is the family Jeep doing? Ethan has been dying for an update!"

"Sarah, I still can't believe you guys gave me a whole ass car. It's crazy nice of you, the Jeep is great, but not getting too much use in the city," I explain.

"It may not get a ton of use around the city, but Ethan and I discussed it immensely. It's a win for me because then you can come home more. Once you get settled of course!" I can practically hear her grin through the phone.

"Sarah, I still think a car is a little much for a gift," I reply.

"Jess, we wanted to do this for you, and I know you, I know you'll pay me back someday in some way. We have Mom's car, and we want you to have a vehicle to come home when and if you need. Ethan and I are saving up to buy a family car in the future someday anyways. You're doing him a favor by keeping the car in the family," she says.

"Okay, I get it," I state, because I could use a car if I want to get home for weekly dinners.

"Yay! Well, anyways, I gotta get back to work hun, but I love you!" she sings into the phone.

I laugh. I wanted to tell her more about last night, but that conversation will have to wait. "Okay, love you, bye!"

I hang up the phone and look around.

I guess it's time to make this place look like a home.

By the time Lindsey comes over, all but one pile of boxes is at least open. There is stuff everywhere and piles of clothes in every corner, but I've made progress.

I fought and won against the urge to sit and doom scroll.

Lindsey brought her dachshund, Scout, over with her.

He goes everywhere with her, even to her bookstore every day. The only place he doesn't go is bars or clubs.

"Alright, order pizza, and then tell me about last night while I put your dishes in the cabinets," Lindsey says after putting her purse down, putting her hair up, and taking her shoes off.

I giggle. "You've got it boss!" I salute her as she throws a wad of bubble wrap at me.

I order and tell her all about how magical Julian was. How we talked about our favorite food, what color we would wear everyday for the rest of our lives, and I even asked him what actor he would pick to play him in a movie.

His answer was Ryan Gosling.

I laughed, and his eyes sparkled.

Lindsey sighs. "You're a damn hopeless romantic in every way. Tell me what happened this morning? What ruined it?"

"It was weird. He just kicked me out. No explanation. He told me I needed to leave." My eyes threaten to water, but I pinch my arm.

I refuse to give that man an ounce of my tears.

I thought he was different. I thought we clicked. I felt like *this could be it* for the first time ever. Turns out, I was horribly wrong. He's just like every other guy I've been with.

"Maybe he's a jerk, but don't let him destroy your self-esteem from one night. You're the best, and deserve the world! Don't let this guy take up your time and energy," she says.

"I know, I'll try. Thanks, Linds." I smile at her.

The pizza arrives, and Lindsey and I eat while unpacking and putting everything away. We finally get to a point where every box is empty, broken down, and by the front door.

All the bubble wrap and garbage is in a trash bag ready to go out.

I turn and smile at Lindsey. "Have I told you lately you're the best?"

"Yes, but you can tell me again." She laughs. "I'm never moving, I forgot how much this sucks." She picks up Scout and kisses him on the head. "We are never moving, buddy."

I chuckle. "Okay, eventually you'll find a man and move babe," I say while reaching over and scratching Scout behind his ear.

"Nope, they can move in with me and Scout. I'm not moving." She stomps her foot down, as if that's final.

She's silly. I hope she finds her person someday.

"Okay, well you're the best, and I love you. I gotta get some sleep! My first day of work is tomorrow." I grab her hand and we jump up and down squealing.

"I'm so excited for you, Jess!" she squeals with me.

"Okay, love you, bye!!" I push her out the door in a loving way.

"See you tomorrow? Can't wait to hear about your day!" she asks.

"I thought you didn't want to see me everyday?" I giggle.

"Well, I have to see you tomorrow!" She laughs too, before turning around and heading down the hall.

I smile as I close the door.

"Thank god, I thought she'd never leave!" Phyllis yells through the wall.

I groan. I'm definitely moving again someday. I refuse to deal with Phyllis forever.

Chapter Six

JULIAN

I'M SITTING AT MY desk in the back of the flower shop. I'm ready to slam my head into the wall. I'm going to need a miracle to get this store to make enough money to not only pay for the employees and costs, but also enough for Jules and I to live comfortably.

Becky, my current lead florist, pokes her head in.

"Hey, our new lead florist is here to start today." She smiles at me.

"Uh okay." I totally forgot. "I'll be right there," I mutter.

"Try not to look so stressed when you meet her. Let's not scare her off right away; I have a good feeling about this one." She smiles and winks at me as she closes the door.

Becky is moving away for love. We've got a little over three weeks left before she leaves, so I really need the person she hired to work out. Especially considering that I don't have a clue how to make floral arrangements myself.

I take a deep breath and compose myself, because Becky is right. I need to be charming and laid back for our new employee.

I stand up and make my way out to the store. I stop dead in my tracks when I hear the most beautiful laugh coming from our new employee. Her back is currently toward me but her long dark hair is curled and cascading down her back. Becky makes eye contact with me and smiles. "Ah! There he is."

The woman turns, and all the oxygen leaves my lungs. I can't catch my breath. It's . . .

"This is Jess." Becky grins wildly.

Jess looks at me, and her face immediately changes from excited and full of hope, to rage. It's a look of pure anger.

Honestly, her anger sends a wave of heat down my spine, and my cock twitches slightly as I remember our night together. I school my features and keep myself calm, cool, and collected. I need to be incredibly professional at this moment.

There is an awkward tension filling the space between us as I reach out my hand to shake hers.

Fuck. It's the only word on repeat in my head.

Her hand grabs mine aggressively. Neither of us says anything.

Becky mumbles, "Uhhh . . . Do you guys know each other?"

"No, well, kind of, we met the other night . . ." I trail off, looking into Jess's eyes.

"Very brief interaction," she snaps, and I get the jab she's insinuating with that one.

Becky laughs. "Well, this is better than I imagined."

Both Jess and I snap our heads in her direction.

"What does that mean, Becky?" I ask.

"Oh, I was just hoping you two would hit it off. I felt like Jess was perfect for you." She smiles at us.

"Becky! We are hiring an employee for my place of business. This isn't *Love is Blind*," I snap.

"Oh, but I do love that show!" Jess smiles at Becky, attempting to ignore me.

I love it too, but I will never admit that out loud in front of these women. It's entertaining as hell while I'm folding laundry at night.

"Well, hi, Jess, I'm Julian. We are very happy to have you here at Blossom Bliss Corner. Truly, we are grateful you moved here for this job, and hope you love it." I smile at her and try to be a professional man, although my current thoughts are anything but professional.

I need to keep it together though; I need this to work. I don't have time to hire and train someone else before Becky moves. So I need to keep it professional; I need to stay focused on the business.

"I'm excited to be here. This is my dream job. I hope you don't mind, but there are a few changes I would love to be a part of. I have some fun ideas to bring in more people." She pulls a pink binder out of her bag, and hands it to me.

I raise an eyebrow at her. "Changes? Already? You just got here."

"I asked her to think up some fun ideas to bring in more people, Julian. You need to bring more people in," Becky snaps at me.

"Ah, okay, very well then," I say.

I glance down and open the pink binder. I hate to say I'm impressed, but I am. Everything is color-coded and organized inside. It's not something I expect to see from a girl who randomly hooks up with men from the bar.

I glance back up to see Becky and Jess watching me. I close the binder. "This looks great, I'll look over it tonight and let you know my thoughts."

Becky smiles. "You guys are going to be great together!" She claps her hands together.

"Oh, we . . . uhm . . ." I stammer.

Jess also stutters some words I can't understand.

Becky laughs. "Why don't you go back to your office, Julian? We've got everything out here. I'll continue to train Jess."

"Ah, okay. Thanks Becky." I salute, turn, and walk back to my office.

Why the fuck did I just salute her?

I've never saluted someone in my whole damn life.

I make my way into my office, close the door, and then slide down it, ass hitting the floor with a thud.

What the fuck just happened?

The girl I'm actively avoiding, the one I thought I had some kind of feelings for and kicked out . . . is now my employee. The same girl I said I would never see again.

I sigh, and shove my head in my hands.

Who did I piss off in this life to deserve this karma?

Chapter Seven

JESS

WELL, FUCK ME SIDEWAYS.

Since when do men own flower shops? I want to crawl into myself and die. How did I already screw up this new life of mine?

Becky is showing me how to use the register and where everything is kept, but my mind is spiraling.

Julian . . . the man I spent my first night in the city with . . . is my boss.

Becky doesn't seem phased by the awkward interaction we just had, so maybe it isn't as bad as I think. Maybe, just maybe, this isn't a big deal.

He kicked me out, so he obviously isn't interested in me. So that's a plus actually, there is no risk of something else happening.

Maybe we can just move on professionally.

I'd be lying, though, if I said I wasn't interested in him. He's even sexier this morning in this flower shop than he was two days ago.

I'd also be lying if I said when I saw his muscular forearms moving to grab the binder from me I didn't have flashbacks to gripping those forearms on either side of my head the other night.

Good god, who am I? I have spent most of my life friend-zoning guys I've slept with, this should be easy for me.

"Think you can ring up a customer? Or do you want me to go over it one more time?" Becky says, breaking through my own thoughts.

Shit, I have no idea what she just said.

"Oh, uhm, do you think I could watch you ring up the first customer today? Before I try on my own? It really helps me to see something visually and in action," I answer.

She smiles. "Of course! I love that you are advocating for your preferred learning style!"

Little does she know, I've just been in my head and don't know what she said. So I need to see it again.

The rest of the morning goes by quickly. A few customers come in, but not as many as I expected. In between customers, Becky and I make some bouquets.

It's my favorite part. I'm sure it's every florist's favorite part, but taking pieces and making something *whole*, something beautiful, makes my heart happy.

It makes me feel like, maybe someday, I'll be whole. Like maybe someday someone will take my broken pieces, combine them with theirs, and make something beautiful.

Something that everyone looks at with wonder, saying "Wow, I want that."

That's a dream, though.

Becky tells me to take a lunch break around noon, when another florist comes in to work.

I run back to the little break room and pull my lunch box out of the fridge.

As I close the fridge door, I hear Julian mumble, "Nice lunchbox."

I look down at the lunch box in my hands. It's my Care Bear lunchbox that I've had forever.

"Oh, are you a big fan of Care Bears?" I ask, giggling.

"Nope," he says. It seems like he wants to say more, but stops himself.

We stare at each other. Him standing in the doorway, and me standing by the fridge.

"Okay, well, this has been an invigorating conversation. I'm going to take my break and eat my lunch now." I turn my back toward him, and take a seat at the small table in here.

I unpack my salad and pour the dressing over it. I put the lid back on and give it a shake.

I hear the fridge open and close, and then listen to the sound of a can opening. Julian walks around and takes a sip of his Diet Coke.

"You'd get better dressing ratios if you mixed it with a spoon or fork," he says, and then takes another sip of his drink.

"Who are you, the salad police?" I grumble.

"I'm just offering some advice," he mumbles.

"Well, thanks," I say with a sigh.

He turns and leaves the break room.

That man is absolutely obnoxious. Making sure nothing else happens between us should be super easy.

By the end of my shift, I'm exhausted. I've done everything part-time for the past seven years. Part-time school, part-time work, my body isn't used to being on my feet for so long. Sure, I spend an hour or so at the gym every day, but I can't remember the last time I was on my feet for eight hours straight. My dogs are barking.

I get back to my apartment and collapse onto my bed. I have a studio, so no couch, and I'm so nervous I'm going to fall asleep often with my bed being the only place to sit and relax. Other than my uncomfortable bar stools of course, but that won't work right now. Right now I need my feet in the upright and locked position.

My phone rings and I groan loudly.

Phyllis yells through the wall, "Just answer, you whiny baby."

I groan again, ignoring Phyllis and I click my phone on.

"Hi little sis! How was your first day of work? I've been itching to call you all day!" Sarah squeals.

"Tell her we miss her!" I hear Ethan shout in the background.

"Miss you guys too," I mumble into the phone.

"Oh, no! What's wrong? Did you not have a good day?" Sarah sounds concerned; I don't want her concerned.

"Nope, I'm just really tired. I'm not used to being on my feet all day." I groan.

Sarah laughs, loudly. "Well, that's for damn sure. Wish you were, could've used some full-time help here a few years ago."

"Not this again," I say as I put my arm over my eyes. I'm defeated. "You know what? I'll call you in the morning, okay? I really am just tired. I love you and appreciate you checking in. It means a lot, sis."

"Okay, but if you need anything, you call! Do you need me to send you some tea? Or coffee beans? That might help!" she asks.

"I'm okay for now, I'll talk to you soon, okay?" I hang up the phone. I know if I don't she will keep asking questions.

I put my phone face down on the bed, and it immediately buzzes with a text. Ugh, what now? I glance at it.

Sarah texted:

> I'm not going to call back, even
> though I want to. Love you, proud of
> you! Xox

I know it'll be a while still, but Sarah will make an amazing mom someday. She has always been a big part of raising me.

I must've dozed off. I wake up to my phone ringing, still in my hand. I look at the alarm clock on my nightstand and it reads 9:00 p.m. *Shit.*

Phyllis yells through the wall again, "That ringtone is shit, answer your damn phone!"

Reminding myself, once again, I need to get sound-proofing.

I roll my eyes and say, "Hello?"

"Hi, Jess! How was the first day?" Lindsey gleefully asks.

"Ugh, Linds, it was awkward," I whine.

"What? Why? You don't love it?" she questions.

"No, I do love it, but do you remember Julian?" I groan.

"The random guy from the other night? The one you went home with? Still frowning at you about that one

Jess, you can't just go home with random guys. What if something happens to you?" she lectures.

"Yes, yes, Linds, I knoooow. Quit being a mom and listen . . . he's my boss," I whisper.

"Dear lord, I knew you were a slut!" Phyllis shouts through the wall.

I ignore her.

"Jess, no. Please tell me you're kidding," Lindsey cries.

"I am not kidding, sadly. He owns Blossom Bliss Corner. He is the owner and my boss. Today could not have been more awkward. You should've seen his face when he saw that his new employee was me," I say, throwing my head down onto my folded arms. I'd stomp my feet if I wasn't worried that Phyllis would never shut up about it.

"I'd be disappointed if my employee turned out to be you!" Phyllis shouts.

"Phyllis, this is an AB conversation, please C your way out!" I shout angrily.

Lindsey quietly laughs.

"It's not funny, Lindsey. This was supposed to be a beautiful new life, now I have an apartment the size of a fish tank, a nosy neighbor who won't stop annoying me, and I accidentally slept with my boss at my dream job. This isn't going well for me." I sigh. "Maybe I should give up and head back to Daisy Ridge, find something else, or go back to working for my sister. I mean, it was good, why did I have to dream about flowers?"

Lindsey laughs. "I don't know babe, sadly we don't always get to decide what we love . . . or who." She sighs. "Jess, you are stubborn, in a good way, and determined. You light up every room you walk into, and I am positive today was not as bad as it is in your head. I guarantee they are looking forward to having you work there."

"I don't know Linds . . ." I whisper.

"I do. I know my best friend is going to show up tomorrow, ready to make that flower shop her bitch. I know she will make that man regret questioning her abilities. She will make him adore her as his employee, and he will beg her to never leave. You will show up and be the best florist, because you are the *best* florist. I believe in you; don't give up on something just because it might be hard," she says.

Tears prick behind my eyes. I'm not a great friend, so I don't know how or why life decided I deserve to have Lindsey as a bestie. But I'm so damn grateful.

"Thanks, Linds, love you," I whisper.

"Anytime babe. Now, do you want some food? I'm heading up the stairs to your apartment." She laughs.

"Oh my god, you're an angel," I cry.

Chapter Eight

JULIAN

I HATE TO ADMIT it, but the binder Jess made is good, really good. After I got home, had dinner with Jules, helped her with her homework, and got her ready for bed, I sat down and started looking through it.

There are all kinds of ideas, neatly categorized. A tab for event ideas, one for daily activities we could offer, a tab for rearranging the store, and more.

I have two immediate favorite ideas. The first being to rearrange and add a 'build your own bouquet bar'. The idea is so easy and fun, and it's also low-cost. Mostly just rearranging and using things we already own.

The other idea I love is to host bouquet-making classes. Being in the city, we get a lot of groups visiting from out of town. Jess has mapped out costs, a schedule for the class, and everything we need to accomplish it. She even has an example scenario for a local book club, who apparently already expressed interest? From what I remember at the bar the other evening, her friend owns Rose Point Books. So I'm sure that is where the interest came from, but it's still a great start.

I close the binder, and go peek in Jules' room to make sure she is cozy and asleep, just as I do every night. It's probably an unnecessary part of my evening checklist, but it calms me down so I can actually sleep.

Tonight I walk over, pull the covers up, and kiss her forehead.

I've made a lot of mistakes in this life, but this little girl will never be one of them. She's everything.

I move out of her room, making sure not to trip over the carefully placed stuffy tea party happening in the middle of the floor, softly closing the door behind me.

I need to shove whatever feelings I have floating around my head for Jess deep down inside of me. I don't want to mess anything up for me and Jules.

I wanted to stay away from Jess after the other night because I'm not ready. Now I have to be around her almost every day. It's going to be hard, but she has great ideas for the flower shop, and I need her to make them a reality. I need Blossom Bliss Corner to succeed, to thrive. I think Jess can be the one to do it, as long as my feelings don't get in the way.

The next morning, Jules and I are running late. She spilled my coffee as we were about to head out the door. It was an accident, of course, so I told her not to worry about it.

There is a small stain on my sleeve from the coffee incident, but nothing the Tide pen in my office drawer can't handle.

We ran out the door, and I somehow got her to school right on time.

I stop at the coffee shop near work to grab a new coffee since mine was lost to Tornado Jules. As I wait in line, I hear the chime on the coffee shop door open. I turn to see Jess walking through the door.

She looks stunning, as always. Her hair is cascading in gorgeous dark waves. Her lips are red and luscious. She has a kind of presence that draws your attention before you even understand why.

She has an air of confidence and she moves with ease, like she knows exactly where she is going without needing to prove anything to anyone. Her eyes scan the room, not looking for anyone in particular, just taking everything in. She looks calm, but curious. There is something in her expression . . . a quiet intelligence, a hint of a smile like she knows a secret the rest of us haven't learned yet.

She isn't just beautiful; she is present. It feels like the whole coffee shop leans into her without realizing it, me included.

Her eyes find mine, and my stomach drops. I get butterflies in my stomach for the first time in forever. Her lips turn up slightly at the corners, like she can't help but smile at me, even though she doesn't want to.

She moves to get in line behind me.

I flex my hands at my sides, because I'm not quite sure what to do. Should I turn around and say something? Or should I be polite and let her cut me? Should I stand next to her?

It's been so long since I've even socialized. I'm not sure what standard protocol is. I glance to try and peek over my shoulder. My eyes meet hers, and now I have to say something or else it's just weird.

"Hey," I say, awkwardly shoving my hands into my pockets.

Hey, is that really all I could come up with? What is it about this girl that makes me so tongue-tied?

She smiles, her entire face gently illuminating. "Hey," she whispers sheepishly.

"Getting coffee before work?" I ask, like Captain Obvious.

"Yep, hopefully this coffee shop doesn't take too long, I would hate to upset my new boss." She smirks, and it shoots a lightning bolt of heat down my spine.

"Oh, new boss, huh? What are they like? Absolutely the worst?" I tease.

"Eh, he's fine for now. Can't really get a read on him yet, but I have high hopes." She laughs, and I can't help thinking that I'd do anything to keep hearing that sound.

I smile at her. Talking to her is so damn easy. Even when I'm so deep in my own head.

"Well, I hope for your sake he ends up being super cool." I laugh. "What kind of coffee do you want? A good employer would buy coffee for the new girl if he happened to see her at the coffee shop."

"Oh, that's really okay . . . I can grab it." She reaches for her card, as we are next in line.

I grab her hand to stop her. "I insist," I whisper.

She looks up at me, and we lock eyes. For a moment the entire coffee shop drifts off, and she's the only person in this room. I look down at my hand realizing I've inadvertently touched her.

I pull away, and flex my hand as if it's been burned. Why the fuck did I touch her? This is going to be a legal nightmare; she's my damn employee now.

I begin spiraling, just now realizing: we've slept together and now she works for me? Is there legal action she can take with that? Am I in deep shit?

Jess clears her throat, removing me from my thoughts.

I look back at her.

"Whatever you're thinking, it's fine, really. And I'll have an iced black tea with honey and a splash of cream." She smiles.

"Tea?" I question.

She laughs. "Are you a coffee snob too? Oh, my sister would just love you. Yes, I just want an iced tea, please and thank you."

"Okay." It's our turn, so I step up to the counter and order Jess her tea first so I don't forget her order. Then I order myself a latte, and pay.

When I turn, Jess is on her phone texting. She glances up at me. "You ordered a hot latte, right?" she asks.

"Uh, yeah, why?" I question.

"Oh, my sister owns a coffee shop, and she's getting ready to open a second location. She has theories about knowing people based on their coffee order. I just want to ask her what a guy ordering a hot latte means." She giggles as she types on her phone.

"Is she going to be mad if you're in a different coffee shop?" I ask.

"Well, considering hers is in a different city, I think she will understand. Although I'm sure she will try to teach me how to make my own tea again next time I go back home." She laughs.

Her phone chimes, and she glances down and laughs.

"What did she say?" I ask, enjoying the sound of her laugh this morning.

She turns the phone to me.

> nothing screams "I fear change" quite like paying six dollars for warm milk with a hint of espresso.

> He really woke up and said, *"I want to feel adventurous, but only in the most bland way possible."*

"She's good," I laugh reading the messages, "and not wrong, I hate change."

Jess laughs too, as the barista calls out our drinks.

We grab them, and turn to head out the door. "Do me a favor, ask her what I should try next time? I actually think I might need a little change in my life."

She smiles, and I know I'm in trouble. Having Jess around all the time is going to be the biggest test my willpower has ever withstood.

Jess and I walk a few doors down together to the store. I open the door for her, and as she passes, it hits me. Soft at first, barely more than a whisper, but her perfume lingers behind her like a secret meant only for me. It's warm, delicate, and impossibly familiar, floral notes mingling with something deeper, like amber or sun-warmed skin.

My breath catches before I even realize it, pulled into the trance she leaves behind. Time seems to slow as the perfume curls around my senses, drawing me in, turning a simple moment into something more.

As she disappears into the store, her fragrance remains a haunting, lovely echo, that leaves me wondering if she noticed my quiet pause.

I turn to see Becky staring at me, a soft smile on her face. Like she knows. She clears her throat, and I all but run inside.

"Morning Becky!" I say, a hint too loud, as I run into the back office as quickly as I can.

The echo of Becky's laugh taunts me all morning.

Chapter Nine

Jess

"How are you feeling today?" Becky asks me as I get started.

I want to say that I'm tired because this schedule is very weird for me, and that I'm confused because her boss is hot and then cold.

But instead I say, "Great! How are you?"

She grins. "I'm very good today! I got word that my offer went through on the house I wanted! I'm so excited to move. Worried about Julian, but hopefully he will be in good hands with you before I leave."

I don't know how to respond to that last part, so I just respond to the first. "Oh, congrats on the house Becky! That's so exciting!"

From what Becky has shared, she is moving with her husband across the country. He actually moved out there two months ago to start his new job, while she got everything situated here. She is in the process of selling their condo here, and hiring me. They've been doing weekend visits here and there. His new job pays a lot more, so she isn't worried about finding a job until she gets there. Once all the ducks are in a row (her words, not mine) she can move to be with him.

It's a small bummer for me because I really like Becky. She's so nice and a joy to work with. I also know that if all my plans are set in motion, hopefully I will be the one hiring someone someday soon. Wouldn't that be amazing?

"Coffee with the boss this morning, huh? I knew you guys would hit it off," Becky says.

"Oh, no. We just happened to go to the same coffee shop, the one a few doors down. I guess I shouldn't be surprised since it's so close to here. We didn't go together though . . ." I correct her.

"Well, still, I think you guys are going to get along really well. I'd bet my life savings on it." She winks at me.

I'm not sure what to say or do in this situation, so I just start getting today's online orders ready for pickup. Our delivery driver will be here in the next hour or so, and I have a lot left to do.

Tucker, our delivery driver, picks up the orders and heads out for the day just as Stephen shows up.

Stephen is a gardener/farmer? I'm not sure his exact title, but he works at the local farm here in Rose Point, Petal Patch Acres. He is the contact that brings our flowers to the shop and delivers them. He is a handsome guy, but seems uninterested in flirting, or at least he wasn't interested in flirting yesterday when I met him.

He actually seems super distracted in general.

He is a massive dude with broad shoulders, blue eyes, and sandy blond hair. He gives Chris Hemsworth vibes honestly.

Stephen looks like a true farm boy in a solid white T-shirt and jeans, unloading our shipment of fresh flowers.

I ask him if he needs any help bringing in the delivery, and he grunts a "no" in response. I look at Becky and shrug. She laughs.

"That's just Stephen for you. Man of few words, always in his own little world. He does a great job, though, and he *will* speak up if he needs something."

"Alright." I laugh. I make a note to take a trip out to Petal Patch Acres on one of my days off. I'd love to see where our flowers are coming from, and what else they offer.

I've heard the farm is an insane tourist attraction at Christmas time too, as they are also a Christmas tree farm that has holiday activities.

The day passes quickly. I don't see much of Julian the rest of the day, and I'm slightly disappointed by it. Although I don't know why. He's a jerkface who kicked me out of his house after a magical night. I need to move on. That stupid drunken orgasm plays on repeat in my head, though.

When I get off work, I text Lindsey.

> We might need a night out on the town, I need to remove an orgasm from my head.

Chill girl, we are going to Brooke and Lucas' engagement party soon. Can you relax and focus on work until then?

> No, I don't think you understand, I have to forget an orgasm, so that I can focus on work.

Jess, your psycho is showing. Get it together bitch. LOL. We will go out Friday, until then I am here if you need casual meals, movie watching, or Scout snuggles.

> Fine. I'll take some Scout snuggles and watching a romantic comedy with my best friend. Please.

Perfect, love you, see you tonight.

Lindsey shows up that night with Scout, a million snacks, and a pint of ice cream. My best friend is gorgeous, even in pajama pants and a baggy T-shirt. Her red hair is piled high on top of her head, and her skin is free and clear of a single blemish.

She's a simple girl, and has been for as long as I've known her. She's the yin to my yang, and sometimes I wonder why she continues to be friends with a brat like me. Lindsey has her shit together, and I'm over here begging for her to help me forget about an orgasm I had with a man the same night that I met him.

I'm grateful for her. I don't think I could've done this epic move to the city without her.

"So what are we watching?" she asks as she grabs us spoons for the ice cream pint.

"I don't know, I want a romantic comedy? Or something to make me cry? Do you have a preference?" I ask.

"Hmmm, is there a romantic comedy movie where the girl accidentally sleeps with her boss?" She laughs hysterically and can barely get the words out.

I grab a pillow and chuck it at her.

She continues laughing. "Okay, sorry, but you asked for it."

I roll my eyes. I pull a blanket out from the storage under my bed and throw it on top of my bed. I hate the idea of eating snacks in my bed, but I don't have a couch. Studio life is fine, until you have a friend over to watch a movie and eat snacks.

Scout jumps up and makes himself comfy on my bed. I sometimes wish I had some kind of pet, but I'm too wild for that life. I can barely take care of myself most days. It would be super selfish of me to own an animal at this point in my life.

My mind wanders to Julian's house ... I saw a fish tank, but it didn't look like it was in use. I wonder if he had a fish die recently.

Lindsey shouts, "Earth to Jess! Come in Jess!"

"What?" I say.

"I asked if you want anything else from over here before I come get comfy?" She laughs. "What are you thinking about so intently?"

"I was wondering if Julian has a fish . . ." I whisper.

She laughs. "Wow, we *do* need to get this orgasm off your mind."

"I told you!"

Lindsey and I both fell asleep halfway through the movie. Luckily, she anticipated that and had set an alarm. So we got a nice early start to our Wednesday. She takes Scout out to go potty, and we get ready for the day. I give her clothes to borrow for work today, which is easy, since she's the boss and can wear whatever she wants.

She throws her hair up in a bun while I meticulously fix my curls to give my hair my old Hollywood glam look.

"You know. . . You can throw your hair up every once in a while without the earth exploding or children dying. It would all be okay." She giggles.

"Gosh, I know, Linds. I just want to look nice. It's my first week at this job. I want to make a good first impression," I explain as I put on my makeup and signature red lipstick.

"A better first impression than sex? I don't think a first impression gets any better than that for a man." She laughs hysterically.

I slap her. "That wasn't my first professional impression, so shut up," I grumble.

Phyllis bangs on the wall. "You two are the most embarrassing and annoying friends I've ever listened to. And that says a lot because I've been alive many years."

I shout back, "At least I have a friend, you old hag!"

"I have friends, you little tramp!" she yells back.

I glance over at Lindsey, and we silently laugh.

"Ready to go?" I ask her.

"Ready!" She smiles.

Together, Lindsey and I walk down to the coffee shop that is by my work. It's on Lindsey's way home anyways. I don't normally get a drink out of the house two days in a row anymore; I'm still adjusting to not getting free drinks from my sister.

But Lindsey insisted, and technically I didn't purchase yesterday's.

She puts Scout in her little bag dog carrier as we walk into the coffee shop and get in line. It's busier than yesterday.

When we get up to the counter, I order my usual iced black tea, and then pause before saying, "And a medium brown sugar latte."

Lindsey's head snaps to mine. "Uh . . ."

I pay and turn to see Lindsey impatiently waiting for me to explain myself.

"It's for . . . Julian. Sarah told me to get him one to try." I grimace.

"Oh, okay," Lindsey mutters. "So we are getting him coffee now, huh?"

"No, it's just, he bought mine yesterday," I stutter.

"He . . . okay . . . why didn't we talk about all this?" She laughs anxiously.

"I . . . There is nothing to talk about, he's my boss. I'm grabbing him a coffee, isn't that what new employees do sometimes?" I grumble.

She laughs again. "I suppose in the movies, although I've never had any of my new employees grab me a coffee . . ."

"Well, then you have shitty employees," I state blatantly.

She snorts. "Whatever you need to tell yourself, babe."

I roll my eyes at her as the barista calls out our orders.

Chapter Ten

JULIAN

THE SHOP ALWAYS SMELLS like eucalyptus in the morning.

It's quiet, the kind of quiet that only exists before customers start showing up either full of love or with broken hearts and last-minute apologies. The light shines soft through the front window, warming up the reds in the tulips.

I'm behind the counter, wrestling with a stubborn roll of kraft paper that keeps unspooling like it's got a personal vendetta against me, when I hear the jingle of the door.

And then I hear *her*.

"Bringer of caffeine, breaker of rules," she sings.

I look up.

She's in a leather jacket and red dress, hair tucked beautifully behind one ear, holding a to-go cup like it's some kind of peace offering, or a weapon. It's hard to tell with Jess.

"You're not scheduled for another twenty minutes," I say, harsher than I intended.

"Yeah, well, you looked homicidal yesterday when you ran out of coffee. Figured I'd come early and spare us all from your misery," she explains.

She sets the coffee down on the counter between us. I stare at it for a beat longer than necessary.

My name's written on the lid. Underneath it, she's drawn a tiny doodle of a rose. A sad-looking one. It's drooping.

"Why is the rose dying?" I ask her.

"Because it's tired, like you." She smiles.

She leans on the counter, watching me with that barely-there smirk that doesn't bode well for my self-control.

She has no idea what she's doing, or she *absolutely* does. Either way, this? This is a problem.

Because she's my employee.

Because I'm her boss.

Because I need her help to make this place better.

Because I'm a *dad*.

Yet every time she says something clever or kind or wildly inappropriate, a part of me starts building some dumb fantasy where none of that matters in my head.

"You know this is wildly unprofessional, right?" I snap.

"What, coffee? Or drawing dying plants on beverage lids?" she asks.

"Yes" is all I can manage to say.

She laughs. "Relax. It's just caffeine. Besides, this is the drink my sister suggested for you to branch out with. Still a latte, just a hint of flavor."

She starts unpacking a crate of marigolds like she didn't just punch a hole through my morning routine.

It's *not* just caffeine. It's her showing up early, and helping.

It's the rose doodle. It's her thinking about me when she stopped for coffee today.

It's her being the person who makes this place feel like more than just work for the first time in forever.

She sets the crate down, and walks off to the back room before I can say anything else. Arms swinging with joy, humming something off-key.

I look down at the coffee.

And I'm smiling again, like an idiot. Like a man who's in serious trouble.

Becky arrived a few minutes after Jess went to the back. I took that as my cue to go into my office for a bit.

I work on our online ordering system. Jess made the suggestion to add our signature flower bouquets to Door-

Dash and Instacart in her binder, so I'm currently looking into the logistics of that. I think it's a great idea, as long as the financial side of it makes sense.

Becky comes and knocks on the door midday.

"Hey boss, I hate to ask for anything, since I only have a couple weeks left, but I have that appointment today, remember? You were going to train our new girl this afternoon?" She speaks softly, like she's trying not to startle a sleeping bear.

Shit. I do remember this conversation. It was back before I knew the new girl was … Jess. Becky has been an angel all these years though, so I need to help her however I can.

"Yep! Totally. What time do you need to leave?" I ask calmly.

"Uh, about fifteen minutes or so?" she mumbles.

"Cool! I'll be out in five." I smile at her, letting her know all is well.

"Thanks, boss," she whispers as she closes the door softly.

I finish up on my computer, run to the restroom, and then go throw my apron on.

"Alright, Becky! Head out! We will see you tomorrow!" I wave, and shoo her out the door.

She laughs. "Already trying to get rid of me?"

"Nope. Never, I wish you would work here for the rest of your life, but I care about you too much to let you. Plus, this isn't the end *yet*. This is just me, making sure you don't miss your appointment."

"Okay, okay," she says with glassy eyes.

"Nope, none of that today. Today you are just leaving for an appointment. Now scram." I chuckle.

She grabs her stuff and heads out the door. Jess is making bouquets at the counter, and looks up to meet my eyes.

She is stunning. It's honestly unfair. I'm not ready to feel this way about a woman. I also can't feel this way about an employee.

She smirks, as if she can read my thoughts.

I clear my throat. "Are you doing okay? Need any extra training on anything specific?" I ask.

"No, I think I'm doing okay." She smiles. "I am curious, though, do you think I could come in early or stay late one day to create the Build Your Own Bouquet Bar? I saw your message that it was approved for me to start implementing."

"Uh, sure. Let me look at the schedule for next week. We can move some things around. I don't want you working overtime at all," I say.

"I really don't mind. I don't have much of a life here yet." She laughs.

"Well, you have at least one friend that I know of . . .and I'm sure you'll be dating soon," I manage to say. The thought sends a wave of nausea to my stomach.

I've only known this girl for like a few days . . . what the fuck do I care if she starts dating?

She laughs. "Oh gosh, Julian, are you trying to ask me about my dating life?"

"No, uh . . . I just meant ..." I stutter.

She laughs. "Relax! I decided after I accidentally slept with my boss before starting my dream job, I should probably take it easy and just get used to Rose Point for a bit."

"Oh, well, that's good?" I ask questioningly. "I am . . . sorry about that," I say quietly.

"For kicking me out after a great night together? Or for the actual night itself?" she asks.

I stare at her for a moment, not sure what to say. The night was amazing in the moment, but I woke up full of regret, and Jess deserves so much more than that.

I open my mouth to form some kind of response, when the door swings open and a customer walks in wailing.

"I messed up! I need flowers and an apology card!" he says with tears in his eyes.

"No problem, we can help with that," I tell him.

"Yep, flowers are meant to say what words can't!" Jess adds with a smile.

I cut Jess off and help him on my own, because I can't help myself. I may not be able to ease the turmoil I feel inside, but hopefully I can make someone else's day better.

The rest of the afternoon goes by quickly. Jess and I help customers, make bouquets, and receive a shipment from Stephen.

I watch Jess try and make conversation and chat with Stephen. It's humorous to me because I've known Stephen for seven years, and the guy has barely said ten words to me. He is a quiet dude who keeps to himself.

Toward the end of my shift, I get a text from David.

> Hey man, we are going out after work Friday for beers. Want to join us?

> Thanks for the invite. I'll talk to my mom about watching Jules, and think about it.

> Cool. Even if you don't want to, I'm here. I can always come watch the game with you on Sunday?

> Thanks man, appreciate it.

I know David is trying to keep me out of my shell, keep me engaged in the real world. I just enjoy being home with Jules more.

Jess closes everything in the store up. She's a natural here. Everything she does makes it seem like she's been doing this her whole life.

"Alright, I'm out. Unless you need something else?" she asks.

"Nope. I think we are good to go. Let me grab my stuff from the office. I can walk you out," I say.

"Oh, you don't have to. It's fine," she replies.

"I insist. Just wait one second." I run back and grab my bag, turn off all the lights, and lock up the back office.

When I come back out, I stop at the sight of Jess twirling a ranunculus in her hand. The shop is dark, but the light from outside frames her silhouette. I can't help but stare for a moment.

I clear my throat to get her attention.

She looks over at me and smiles. "Sorry, I was just thinking about this ranunculus. It feels too beautiful to last, you know?" she whispers.

There is a long pause, because I know she isn't talking about the ranunculus. I'm unsure of what to say next.

She shakes her head, washing away her thoughts. "Sorry, are you ready to go?" she says softly.

"Yeah," I whisper, even though I'm not ready. I don't actually want to leave this view.

We head outside in silence. I lock up the door behind us, and turn to the street. "Where are you parked?" I ask her.

"Oh, I just walked since I'm just around the corner," she mumbles.

"You walked?" I ask.

"Yeah, but I'm just around the corner, it's not far. I'll see you tomorrow." She waves.

I grab her hand and pull her toward my car. "Come on, I'll drive you home."

I hold her hand the entire way to my car. I'm not sure exactly why I do it, but I know that it feels right. I'm sad to let it go when I open the passenger door and she climbs in.

Something about Jess' skin on mine just feels undeniably like exactly where I'm meant to be.

Chapter Eleven

JESS

I'm in Julian's car. And not only that, but he held my hand on the way here. I have no idea why he did that, but I'm not complaining.

He doesn't drive what I thought he would, he drives a Toyota Camry. I don't know much about cars, but I know this one isn't brand new, but it also isn't old. Maybe five or six years old? I don't know. Not what I pictured him in, though.

I have such mixed feelings about Julian. He seems like a nice guy. I watched him interact with customers this afternoon, and it was odd.

He was smiling, like actually *smiling*.

Not that stone-faced glare he gave me when he told me to leave his house that morning. Not the silence that filled the room after everything we'd done, like I was some kind of mistake he needed to erase.

But he was there, in this sunlit shop, handing a little girl a daisy like he's some kind of soft-hearted poet. His voice was gentle. Then two minutes later he's laughing with an older gentleman, helping him find the perfect anniversary bouquet.

Did I hallucinate that morning?

Because that morning, after everything . . . after the heat and closeness and the way he whispered my name like it meant something . . . he didn't even look me in the eye. Just told me I should go, like I was an inconvenience to him.

And today he's giving kindness out like petals.

What the hell?

Did I just catch the worst version of him, or was *I* the exception to his warmth? And not in a good way.

Is this real? This tenderness with others? Or is it just a performance?

Or, and here's the worst thought, maybe he's actually kind. Maybe he's this guy, the one I saw today who seems to be good with everyone.

Just not with me.

Maybe I'm the exception.

Julian is staring at me. "You ok?" he asks.

"Yep, sorry, zoned out there for a second." I put my hair behind my ear, and stare at the windshield in front of me. I can't meet his eyes right now.

I feel sick, and I don't know why. I've been with plenty of guys, and I've never cared. Why do I care about this man? I only spent one night with him.

"Where am I going?" he asks.

"Oh, right, sorry. Do you know where the Orchid Heights Apartment building is? On Stem Street?" I ask him.

"Yeah, I know where that is." And he starts driving.

We ride in silence around the corner. It isn't a far drive. He pulls up to my building, and pulls out his phone, texting vigorously.

"Okay, well, thanks!" I mumble, although he doesn't seem to care. He's too busy looking at this phone. "Bye." I climb out of the car and close the door.

He rolls down the passenger side window, and yells, "Sorry, bye Jess, see you tomorrow!"

I wave, and head into my building.

When I make it upstairs and to my door, I want to cry, but I keep it together. Phyllis pops her head out as I'm unlocking my door.

"Was that the boss you accidentally slept with?" she grunts.

"Phyllis, mind your damn business. Don't you have anything better to do? What are you, the building guard staring out your window?" I snap.

"I don't have my glasses on, but he might be pretty cute," she says, and then slams her door.

I sigh.

I know you're supposed to be polite to the elderly, but that lady drives me absolutely insane.

I head inside and close the door.

I text back and forth with Lindsey for a while, chatting about our day.

Then I text Sarah and my Dad, to keep them updated. It's weird being away from them for so long.

I lay on my bed, and want to close my eyes. I'm so tired, but I know I shouldn't. If I do, my sleep schedule will continue to be a mess.

I force myself to sit up, and turn on the TV.

My phone beeps, and it's a group text with Brooke and Lindsey.

> Brooke: Don't forget that next Friday night is my engagement party with my family. It's small, but I want you both there as my bridesmaids. <3 xoxo.

I read the message a second time, because I've never met Brooke's family before, but Lindsey has. One could say Lindsey knows her family really well.

From what I know, Lindsey dated Brooke's brother back in high school and early college years. Lindsey says he moved away and there is no bad blood, but the way Lindsey avoids talking about him at all costs, she's probably freaking out.

I text Lindsey separately.

Is her brother going to be there? Are you ok? Do we hate him? I need the info, don't make me go into this blind.

I flip channels trying to find something to watch, but I'm getting antsy. I can't just sit here. I turn off the TV and get up, throw my shoes back on and head out the door.

I start walking down the street, and realize I have no idea where I'm going. I look both ways and decide I can use some groceries and stuff at home, so I go to the nearest store.

I walk in the supermarket and grab a cart.

Lindsey texts me back, so I look down at my phone and accidentally bump my cart into someone else's.

"Oh my gosh! I am so sorry," I cry.

"No worries sweetie! If I had a phone at your age, I probably would have done the same thing at one point!" I look up and spot an older woman smiling at me and holding a little girl's hand.

The little girl is adorable. There is something familiar in her expression, but I don't know any kids, especially not in Rose Point, so there is no reason for me to know her.

She smiles up at me too.

"Well, I am so sorry. I was distracted by a friend's engagement. I feel bad," I mumble.

"Seriously, nonsense dear, it's fine," the old woman says.

"You're really pretty!" the little girl shouts up at me.

I kneel down so my face is level with hers. "And you, my dear, are gorgeous! Look at this dress, it is the epitome of fashion!" I tell her.

She grins at me. "Thank you," she says as she curtsies.

I stand back up. "I am so sorry again," I tell the older woman.

"Really, we are happy as clams! I only wish someone like you would date my son. Are you single?" she asks.

I laugh. "I am incredibly single, but currently not dating. I need to take a break from that silliness."

The little girl laughs. "Grandma! You can't ask strangers to date my dad!"

"Well, with a face like yours, I'm sure your dad is very handsome." I turn back to the woman. "I am so flattered, truly, but I'm kind of a mess. I just moved here, and don't really have my life together yet." I shrug.

"Who has their life together in their twenties? Actually, I don't even know anyone who had their life FULLY together in their thirties. You're young, and my son needs to learn how to have fun again!" She pulls out a sheet of paper from her enormous bag, scribbles a number on it, and hands it to me. "This is his phone number, if you change your mind!" She winks at me, grabs the little girl's hand and heads off toward the register.

The little girl waves at me aggressively with her free hand. I wave back, and laugh.

I'm glad I ran into them. I won't be texting her son, but it was a fun interaction. That little girl is adorable. I throw the scrap of paper in my pocket, and start shopping.

Chapter Twelve

JULIAN

"WE'RE HOME!" MY MOM shouts as she enters my house with Jules.

My mom has been picking Jules up after school this week, and keeping her through the early evening so I can stay and get some work done. Today she texted that they were going to get some groceries and make dinner at my house.

I came home to an empty house, which was sad, but I'll admit, kind of nice.

I actually got to sit down for a minute.

I jump up and Jules comes barrelling into my arms!

"DAD! You're home!" she shouts as she squeezes me in a big hug.

"Of course, Jujubee. I'll always come home." I give her three tiny squeezes, our way of saying I love you.

"Grandma gave your phone number to a pretty lady at the store." She smiles up at me.

My head whips to my mother. "What?"

"Oh, relax, Julian. You could use some of her spunk in your life, plus she was a very pretty lady," my mom explains.

"Mother. . ." I scold.

Jules interjects, "She wasn't just pretty, she was amazing! I loved her. I hope she calls you."

I look at Jules. "Sweetie, even if she does . . . you can't just meet strangers at the store," I explain.

"Why not?" Jules asks.

"Yeah, where else are you supposed to meet people, Julian?" my mother questions.

"I . . . uh . . . I don't know. Just places," I say.

"Well, what's the difference between meeting someone at the store or meeting them at school?" Jules asks.

I clap my hands together. "Jules, why don't you go wash up in the bathroom before helping Grandma cook?"

"Are you trying to make me leave so you can yell at Grandma?" she asks.

"Jujubee. Go wash," I scold.

"Ugh, fine," she replies, and takes off down the hall.

I turn to my mom. "You can't do that to Juju. If I do decide to date, which is unlikely, she cannot be involved. You can't get her hopes up like that."

"It was a funny interaction. Her cart bumped into mine, and she was so sweet talking to Jules, I just had to seize the opportunity," she explains.

"Mom. Just promise you won't do things like that again. Besides, this woman could be a serial killer for all you know." I frown.

"Julian, you worry too much." She chuckles as she ties the apron she keeps at my house around her waist.

I'm laying in bed staring at the ceiling. My thoughts drift to Jess. Her gorgeous eyes, the corner of her mouth, the way she moaned that first night in my bed.

I physically slap myself across the face. I need to fucking get it together.

My phone chimes, I look at the clock, 10:38 p.m. Who the hell is texting me this late?

I pick up my phone, but it's a number I don't have saved.

> Sorry for the late message, I met your mom at the store today. Wasn't going to message, but your kid was so damn cute. If you ever need a babysitter, feel free to reach out. I have references I can send!

I'm honestly relieved she didn't ask about me or a date. However, talking to me about my kid, when I don't know her. It's weird. I hate it.

I close the message and set my phone back on my night-stand.

I start thinking about tasks for the morning, and getting Juju out the door for school. I wish I had a way of knowing if Jess wants coffee tomorrow . . .

It's 12:58 on Thursday, and Jess is giving me a hard time for telling her that lavender is one of my favorite scents.

"Lavender? How original, you and every yoga mat in the world!" she cackles.

"I don't even do yoga! What on earth are you talking about? Lavender is a common favorite," I defend.

"It smells like a spa gift basket from the clearance aisle! People post lavender on their Instagram stories and then forget to drink water for two days, but claim they are a wellness influencer!" she rants.

I laugh, because I can't help it. Jess and her soapbox about the scent of lavender is hilarious.

The store phone rings, and we both jump. I hear Jess answer, and then mumble, "Uhm, just a minute."

She sets the phone down and speed walks toward me. "Uhm, Julian, there is an elementary school on the phone for you."

"Shit." I run to the phone.

"Hello?"

"Hi Julian, it's Dr. Kate from the nurse's office. Jules threw up in her P.E. class, and is sitting here with me," she explains.

"Ah, crap. Okay, uhm, give me a few minutes to sort things out, either my mom or I will be there as soon as possible," I say.

"No problem, she's going to lie down with some Saltines for now," she says with a chipper tone, as if she didn't just throw a wrench in my whole day, and probably my tomorrow as well.

"Great!" I hang up.

I run to the back and dial my mom. I explain the situation to her.

"Normally I wouldn't ask, but Becky is out right now, and the only person working is my new employee," I add.

"I'll go grab Jules, but I have somewhere to be right when you're done at work today. Can I meet you at the store when you're closed?" she asks.

"Yeah, thanks Mom, you're a lifesaver. I owe you. Text me when you've got her." I hang up.

I rush back out front because I realize I've left Jess out there alone.

When I come out, of course, she's fine. She's helping a man order flowers with ease.

I stand back and admire her for just a moment. I know I shouldn't, but I can't help it. She's breathtaking. Her dark hair shines in the sunlight that pours through the store windows. She has a skirt with tights underneath, heeled boots, and a cozy sweater. She looks sexy and professional, and makes it slightly hard to focus.

She finishes up the transaction, smiles warmly at him, and tells him, "Have a wonderful day!"

She turns to look at me, and her warm smile turns to a frown. "Everything okay?" she asks.

"Yeah, yeah, it will be fine," I mumble. I realize quickly that I told my mom to bring Jules here ... and Jess is here.

I'm panicking. I need to get Jess out of the store, or tell my mom to meet me at home. Except I can't do either of those things. Jess is supposed to close tonight, and I can't leave her here alone to close her first week.

She must have seen some kind of worry on my face because she walks over and puts her hand on my arm. "Are you sure? I can help."

That's exactly what I don't want. I don't want help, specifically her help.

I step back. I can't have her hand on me. It's too comforting, and she can't be the one to comfort me. She's my employee.

"I ... uh ..." I'm stuttering and mumbling. I blurt out, "I have a kid."

She looks confused, and then she looks angry, but she says nothing.

"I . . . have Jules. She's six, and she is currently sick at school, so my mom is picking her up, and bringing her here around close . . ." I'm rambling. I'm nervous. Why am I nervous?

"Okay," she mumbles.

"Okay?" I question.

She looks confused again. "Are you . . . I'm sorry . . . Is there a . . . mother?" she asks.

And there it is, the question I worried about when I thought about the idea of dating. The question I can't bring myself to answer. My kid doesn't have a mother, and that eats me alive. Especially when I have the best mom and can't imagine my life without her.

I try to breathe, but the walls feel like they are closing in.

The door chimes, and a customer walks in.

Jess gives me a somber look before walking over to help her. I overhear the woman asking about flowers for a wedding. Perfect, that will take a while.

I walk over to the station where bouquets are made. I pick up a loose peony, and twirl it in my hand. It calms me. It's been something that has calmed me for a while. Twirling an individual flower between my palms and focusing on my breathing.

I never thought I would like someone again, and as much as I hate to admit it, I like Jess. It's unstoppable.

I breathe in through my nose and out through my mouth, trying to calm down. It's the only thing the therapist taught me that's stuck with me all these years.

I think about things that make me happy, calming myself down so I can start thinking logically and rationally.

When I get my heart rate down, I start to rationalize with myself. Jules doesn't know Jess, but Jules has met my other employees. Jules is as much a part of this flower shop as I am.

She's six, so she won't pick up on the fact that I find Jess attractive. She won't know I'm secretly admiring Jess.

It's fine that they will meet today, because it changes nothing for Jules.

I'm calm now, or as calm as possible.

I'm anxious and sick over the fact that I have to ask my mom to pick up my sick little girl. I want to be there for her. I want to be the one to pick her up and comfort her.

And I hate asking for help.

Jess continues to show the woman options for wedding floral packages.

I get back to work. Jess and I have been getting "Build Your Own Bouquet Bar" situated and ready to begin on Monday.

I keep rearranging to prepare.

While I rearrange, I think about what I'm going to say to Jess. I know she is asking because of our night together. It's only fair that I answer her question.

I practice what I'm going to say over and over in my head. I'm so deep in my thoughts, I miss the fact that Jess has finished up with the customer, and has come back over to me.

I startle, and she laughs. It's reserved like she was trying not to, but comes out anyway.

"I'm sorry, I . . . I haven't . . . gosh, I was practicing what I was going to say in my head, but I can't seem to get the right words out," I mumble.

"Then don't try to be right, just say words," she says, smiling.

"Hannah, my . . . uh . . . she passed, about five years ago. I haven't . . . been with anyone since, until, well, until you. I haven't done this before. It's why I panicked the night after we, uhm, well, you know." I get choked up, and it's embarrassing for me. I take a deep breath and try to pull it together.

"Jules, she's my everything, I just . . ." I whisper.

"I get it, no need to explain more. I will be nothing more than a solid and amazing employee when they come in." She rubs her hand down my arm.

It's that same comforting feeling. I immediately feel like I can breathe easy again. Although I know it won't last, Jess just makes everything better. She's crazy and chaotic. But she's confident and really makes me feel like I'm on solid ground, when most of the time I just feel like I'm floating around aimlessly.

I smile at her, and she smiles back, and then we break apart and get back to work. We don't talk about it again.

The hours pass quickly, as they always do in the store.

We close up and start cleaning when there is a knock on the locked front door. I see my mom and Jules, and run over to unlock it and let them in.

Jules runs in and gives me a big hug, doing three tiny squeezes.

"How are you feeling, Jujubee?" I ask.

"Great!" she shouts.

"Great? I thought you were sick?" I ask.

My mom laughs. "Me too, but I think she just went a little too hard in P.E. because she's been perfectly fine since I picked her up."

My mom gives me a look and smirks.

Jess comes around the corner with the mop bucket and mop, when Jules' whole face lights up.

"It's the pretty lady from the grocery store!" she yells.

I whip my head around to Jess.

Jess starts laughing. "Oh my goodness! Hi, you!"

My mom and I share a look, and I just know she's about to say something horrible.

"Why, Julian, you did not tell me your new employee was a gorgeous, sweet girl, in an age range appropriate for you . . ." She winks at me.

OH GOD.

"Well, Mother, this is my *employee*, Jess," I snip.

Jules jumps up and down. "She's my favorite!" She runs over and gives Jess a hug.

Jess, to my surprise, hugs her back and whispers, "You don't look sick."

My mom laughs, and Jules grins up at Jess, and then turns back to me. "Can I pick a flower, Dad?"

"Ooooh I've got something better!" Jess says, grabbing Jules' hand and walking around the corner.

Mom whispers to me, "Well, I've got to go, but I can't wait to see how this plays out."

"I don't know what you're talking about, she's my *employee*, and there is nothing to *play out*." I glare at her.

She pats my arm. "Sure, sure, sweetie. See you tomorrow!"

I walk around the corner and Jess is at the counter making something. Jules sits on the counter kicking her feet, watching Jess with her undivided attention.

Jules tells Jess about throwing up in P.E. and playing freeze tag at recess.

For a moment, my heart flutters with something I haven't felt in a long time: hope.

Chapter Thirteen

JESS

JULIAN HAS A KID.

It came as a shock, but honestly made me feel like he might not be the huge dickhead I thought he was.

My dad probably would have kicked a woman out before Sarah and I got home back in the day. If he actually had someone to help. My dad didn't have a whole lot of help around. Luckily, he had a small town full of folks who would always help a neighbor, but definitely not anyone who could watch us overnight.

Maybe Julian still would've kicked me out though, who knows. The man is hard to read, but I could tell he was struggling earlier.

Jules sits on the counter next to me talking a mile a minute. You'd think the kid hadn't spoken to another human all day. She tells me about some boy in her class who lost a tooth, and how the cafeteria meatballs are not her favorite.

The way her brain swings from one subject to the next makes me laugh.

I don't have a whole lot of experience around kids, but when she said she wanted a flower, I immediately had a fun idea.

My love for flowers all started with flower crowns. When I was young I used to make them from flowers in the park.

I would bring all the flowers home and make crowns for my stuffed animals, and we'd have a tea party.

Making this flower crown for Jules brings me back and makes me feel like a kid again. I put together the last little bit and then present it to Jules. "TA-DA!"

The smile on her face widens, and her eyes light up with excitement.

"JESS! It's amazing!" she shouts.

"A beautiful crown for a beautiful princess!" I place it on her head, and she leaps off the counter.

She runs away, yelling, "I'm going to go look in the mirror!"

I laugh and turn around to head back to the mop I left behind. Julian is standing there staring at me. I can't quite read the expression on his face.

"Thank you," he chokes out.

"Of course! She's the cutest." I walk past him and start mopping.

I mop the whole front half of the store before Jules and Julian come out and start wiping down counters. Jules looks so happy to be helping him, and I can't help but smile.

I always loved helping my dad as a kid. I feel an odd connection to Jules, just based on the pure fact that we both lost our mother at a young age. I also feel guilty. My dad never moved on from my mother, at least not that I know.

I feel like I might have taken advantage of the situation that night with Julian, but it felt like he wanted it too. I feel guilty that I've been calling him an asshole this whole time, when the reality is he was just trying to protect what he has.

I still think he could've handled it better, but I get it now.

I don't feel the sting of rejection quite like before.

However, I have this small bit of sadness in me as well, because I need to leave Julian the fuck alone. I can't be with him. He's my boss, he has a kid, and he was married. As magical as our night together was, I need to stop thinking about it.

I'm sure I'll find another top-tier orgasm again someday.

Later that night, Lindsey and Scout are hanging out in my apartment again. Lindsey is making me dinner, because she is "sick of my girl dinner shenanigans."

Here I thought a slice of cheese, Diet Coke, and beef jerky were perfectly fine along with the occasional peanut butter and jelly sandwich.

According to Lindsey, though, I need to be healthier.

Lindsey runs around my tiny kitchen cooking, while I cuddle Scout on the bed watching *Love Island*.

People think I'm crazy for hooking up with losers, but the people on this show are completely out of control, all making out with each other. I could never; well, maybe I could, I don't know.

At this point, I think I just have issues. I've always just hooked up with guys and not really gave a shit. The last guy before Julian told me he was hooking up with multiple girls in my small town and I just smiled and said, "Cool."

Like, that should have bothered me, but it didn't. I told myself it was because he wasn't the one. But maybe it's just me. Maybe there is no "one" for me.

Scout makes my day better every time he comes to visit with Lindsey. I've never met a more chill dog. He's happiest being with Lindsey, whether that means hanging out in her purse or sleeping amid the shelves in her store. Just being around him makes my anxiety melt away. I rub his floppy ears, boop his little nose, and look over to Lindsey making herself at home in my kitchen. I can tell she's gearing up for something as she asks me how work is.

"It's . . . good," I respond.

"Just, good?" she pries.

"I mean, I like my boss, who I had the best orgasm of my life with. I genuinely woke up in his bed one morning thinking he might be the one. And it turned out he has a kid and this whole trauma-filled past. PLUS, he's my boss. I can't like him. I can't be with him. I just can't." I sigh. "The job itself is awesome, though. I'm finally working with flowers. I love the customers, and I feel like I'm making a difference in the shop."

Scout curls himself further into my lap, while Lindsey stinks up this tiny studio with all her seasonings and bacon.

I carefully remove Scout from my lap and place him on the bed. I get up and move to one of the two windows this apartment has, and open it up.

"You're stinking up the place!" Phyllis shouts through the wall, pounding on it as she does.

"I don't care, we have to eat, get over it!" I shout back.

"Why can't you just have your sad, lonely peanut butter and jelly again?" she yells.

I roll my eyes, and Lindsey laughs.

"Phyllis, would you like some chicken?" Lindsey asks.

"Don't be nice to her! She's a bitch," I snap at Lindsey.

"Ugh, chicken!" Phyllis shouts, "No thanks, I'm ordering pizza." We can hear her shuffling away from the wall.

"Well, Phyllis and I agree on one thing." I laugh.

Chapter Fourteen

JULIAN

I LAY IN BED staring at the ceiling fan. I should be asleep, but I can't seem to fall into slumber. Jules didn't stop talking about Jess all night.

How Jess is so pretty and kind. How Jess made her a flower crown, and how cool is that. How Jess is so funny; she told Jules the funniest joke.

Jules is in love, and I can't say I blame her.

Damn it. This wasn't supposed to happen. I had a plan: work, raise my kid, sleep, and repeat. Love was done, over. Tucked away with the baby clothes and the photo albums I don't pull out anymore.

And then she showed up.

Not like a movie. There was no slow-motion, no sound-track. Just her laugh—sharp, honest, like it didn't care who was listening. And I felt something shift. Something I've been keeping bolted shut since . . . well, since I had to.

I shouldn't feel this way, not now. Not when I've finally built a life with some damn structure. My kid depends on me. I don't get to be reckless. I don't get to want things, at least not for myself.

But there she is, making my daughter a flower crown and making her laugh. My kid's looking at her like she hung the moon. I should be scared of that—hell, I *am* scared of that. Because I know what happens when you love someone. I've done the math, and I've patched the holes. I don't want to do it again. I don't want that for Jules.

And yet . . . I keep looking at her like an idiot, and listening for her voice. Wondering what she's thinking when she goes quiet. Wondering if she notices the way I linger when she says goodbye.

God, this really wasn't the plan.

I don't want to need anyone. Needing leads to nothing good in my opinion. But my heart keeps saying, what if this is different? What if she's the one person who doesn't leave?

Or what if I'm just setting us both up to fall?

I should just fire her, or ignore her. I should protect what's left of me and my family. But part of me—some stubborn, reckless part—wants to believe that maybe . . . just maybe . . . this time doesn't have to end.

And that terrifies me more than anything.

The next day, I take Jules to school, explaining to the nurse she must've just overdid it in P.E. class because she was more than fine the rest of the day.

We have a nice laugh, and as I'm about to leave, she stops me.

"Oh! Julian, one more thing, I'm getting married!" she squeals, showing me her engagement ring.

"Wow! Congratulations!" I say enthusiastically. It's somewhat fake, of course, because I don't know her or her fiancé. I am genuinely unaware of why this concerns me.

"Jules said you own Blossom Bliss Corner? I was curious if I could schedule a time over the upcoming break to come in and discuss floral arrangements for the wedding?" she asks.

"Oh! Of course!" I pull out my wallet and whip out a business card. As I hand it to her, I explain, "Just shoot me an email, we can schedule something with my lead florist. You'll love her, and I'll make sure we get you a great discount. You deserve it, taking care of all these germy kiddos!" I smile politely.

"Ah! Thank you so much! I will reach out!" She jumps up and down slightly. I wave and head out to work.

When I arrive at work, Becky greets me, and I look around the room for Jess before I can even help it.

"She's off today," Becky says with a smirk.

"What? Who?" I try to play dumb. I don't need Becky feeding into anything, since nothing can happen.

Becky laughs. "Oh, you know, Jess. Today is her day off."

"Ah, okay, so is someone else here working today?" I ask, brushing it off like I'm not immediately disappointed to hear Jess isn't here.

"Yep, Mindy is in the back, grabbing some more florals for the "Build Your Own Bouquet" wall Jess made. People have been loving it." She laughs. "Of course, only when she is here to help them, because everyone seems to just adore her."

I grumble.

Jess is wild and immediately draws you in with her confidence and utter joy for life. I'm not surprised people are loving her.

I'm not going to tell Becky any of that, though.

She laughs, as if she can read my every thought.

"Well, since no one here should need my help for a few hours, I'm probably going to run over to Petal Patch Acres. I need to chat with Stephen about the deliveries for next season. I can't believe we are already planning for fall and winter, when it's still so hot out," I state.

Becky laughs. "You've said that every year."

"Well, it's my least favorite part about this job, that's for sure. I hate planning ahead like that," I groan.

"You know who would probably love to do it? Who would probably happily take that task off your hands?" she cackles.

"She just started here, Becky, she doesn't know what she is doing yet. What if it doesn't work out and we have to let her go?" I whine.

Becky full-blown bends over with laughter. "You're a hoot. That girl isn't going anywhere. She's perfect for this place, and in her first week here, we've already doubled our sales from this time last year. I knew what I was doing hiring her. Don't question me."

"Whatever, I'm going to head over to Petal Patch. I'll be back in an hour or two. Call if you need me." I roll my eyes and groan as I head out the door.

Not liking Jess is really hard when every person in my life keeps going on and on about how much they adore her.

But I know the truth: she's captivating, but wild. Jules and I don't need wild in our life, we need stability.

Chapter Fifteen

JESS

IT'S MY FIRST DAY off since I started, and I slept in. It was magical. Phyllis, of course, woke me up by banging on my wall and asking if I was going to sleep away my youth, or get my ass up and enjoy life.

Which was rich coming from a lady I've never seen leave her apartment.

Anyway, even Phyllis can not rain on my parade today. I'm heading to Petal Patch Acres, as I promised myself I would do on my first day off. I really want to see where all the florals are grown, and what we may be missing out on.

I won't mention anything for a bit, if there is something I think we should add. I don't want to come on too strong or get too pushy.

Honestly, I'm just excited to be around florals outdoors again. Hopefully, see them in full bloom. I've been making arrangements inside for so long now, I'm excited to get outside.

I pull up in the Jeep and park in the visitor parking, realizing this place is huge. There is an entrance to the garden, a path to "Mistletoe Meadows," and a little shop, all near the parking lot.

I put my sunglasses on and look down at myself. I knew there would potentially be a lot of outdoor walking, so it's the first time in a very long time I've dressed down.

Black biker shorts, a black and white striped top, and a chambray button-down long sleeve tied around my waist if I get chilly. I left my hair down for now, but brought a hair tie in case it gets unruly. I bend down and tie my Nike tennis shoes laces. As I come up, I'm greeted by Julian.

He's staring down at me with the grumpiest look on his face, as if I've just ruined his whole fucking day.

"What are you doing here?" he demands.

"Why, hello to you, too!" I say cheerfully. "It's a beautiful day for a walk through a garden. Isn't it?"

His face turns down in a frown. "It's your day off," he snaps.

"Yes, so I think I'm allowed to do whatever I want? Like, go for a walk in the garden?" I cross my arms in front of me.

I'm feeling self-conscious right now, without a dress and a full face of makeup, but I'll be damned if he is going to ruin this magical day for me.

We stand there just staring at each other in a stand-off.

"Well, if you'll excuse me, I have a garden calling my name," I grumble.

"I guess I'll walk with you," Julian mumbles.

"You really don't need to," I say.

"It's fine, Stephen can't see me for another twenty minutes anyway," he says softly.

"Oh, okay." I grab my water bottle and fanny pack out of the Jeep.

"I didn't picture you driving a bright red Jeep," he questions.

"And why the hell not?" I snap.

"Jeep doesn't really scream Jess . . . at least not from what I know," he states.

"Well, you're right, it was my sister's boyfriend's. They gave it to me when I moved. I didn't pick it out, but it works great," I explain.

"Ah, okay. Ready?" he asks.

"I guess," I whisper.

We head toward the entrance, and I follow Julian into the garden entrance. We walk down a dirt path that winds around the hill where the entrances are on top of. When we turn the corner, the view takes my breath away.

Flowers for miles, and a little stream that goes in every direction. There is a small waterfall in the distance.

"Wow," I whisper.

"Most people wouldn't guess this is here," he whispers.

I don't know why we are whispering. There is no one around, and it's a damn shame, because this is hands down the most beautiful view I've ever seen.

The sunlight spills soft light over rows of carefully tended roses, topiaries, and stone arches. It's quiet, except for the distant hum of bees and the occasional birdcall.

We begin walking again.

"This pathway is aggressively unpaved," I say harshly.

"It's a *garden*, not a flower shop. What did you expect?" Julian laughs.

Julian laughing in a beautiful garden may be my new favorite moment in life, although I wish it wasn't.

I collect myself and my feelings.

I stop again when we reach the peonies. It's rare to see peonies in bloom like this. I admire them for a minute before turning around to see Julian watching me.

We hold each other's gaze a minute too long, when a garden employee walks by, distracting both of us. We both step back quickly to let her through.

"Morning, Julian!" she says with a smile.

"Morning, Mags," he replies.

She continues walking.

"I enjoy coming here, although I'll never admit that to anyone else. I do like this place, though." He looks out over the garden.

"I mean, how could anyone not like it?" I whisper.

"I like coming here when scheduling spreadsheets and finances make me feel like I'm in trouble." He laughs while looking at the peonies I was just admiring.

"So like, every day? Cause you're always in trouble. You just pretend you're not." I nudge his shoulder and giggle.

There's a long, awkward silence before I say, "I didn't come here to run into you. I didn't even know you came here. I just wanted to see where the flowers come from. Plus, you know Stephen is such a mystery, I had to see where the man works." I laugh.

He laughs. "It's fine, Jess, I'm not complaining."

"You know this is weird, right? Us. Alone. Outside work," I finally say.

"Yeah, but it doesn't have to be. We're just a couple of coworkers accidentally running into each other, in a beautiful garden," he says, and then takes a big drink from his water bottle.

"Yeah, two coworkers who have seen each other naked, and given each other spectacular orgasms." I laugh.

Julian chokes on his water, and starts coughing aggressively.

"What? It's true, unless the orgasm wasn't as good for you as it was for me." I smirk.

"Jess!" he shouts between coughs. "Dear god. Be quiet."

I laugh harder, because I love seeing him all flustered.

I turn around to see a stunning greenhouse, and I get so excited. I've never actually seen a real greenhouse in person.

"Oh my god! A greenhouse!" I shriek, pointing it out to Julian.

I walk over, realizing it's empty.

My heart sinks. "It's empty," I whisper, pressing my hands and face up against the glass to look in.

"Yeah, it's been empty for a while. The person who used to tend to it left a few years back. It hasn't been filled since," Julian explains.

"What a damn shame. I've never actually seen a real greenhouse before. I bet it used to be beautiful . . ." I say as I gently pat the side of it.

Julian looks at his watch. "It's time for me to meet with Stephen. Did you want to come say hi to the mystery man?"

"Sure!" I say.

We walk back toward the entrance. It's familiar; our steps in unison and the quiet garden surrounding us. It's the kind of feeling I always wanted, feeling comfortable in the silence with a man.

Yet there is this nagging voice in my head, chanting "This can't happen. This doesn't work. He needs someone more serious than you. Someone with their shit together. Jules needs a mom, not you."

That voice makes me nauseous.

We walk up the hill, and when we reach the top, Stephen is there waiting. I wave happily at him.

He just stands there with his arms crossed.

"Wow, I finally met someone grumpier than you," I whisper to Julian.

"What is she doing here?" Stephen asks Julian.

"Well, hello to you!" I say.

"She just happened to be here admiring your garden while I was waiting for our meeting. However, she is my lead florist, so please treat her with respect, Stephen," Julian says. His tone at the end is somewhat harsh, but Stephen still doesn't seem fazed.

An employee comes over in jeans and a Petal Patch Acres shirt. She's adorable, and I immediately love her. She's got wild blonde curls, and just the way she walks up to Stephen tells me I'm going to like her.

"You forgot to order the new Christmas ornaments on the last order!" She smacks Stephen's chest.

Stephen grits his teeth together and closes his eyes.

"We've got plenty of time, Taylor. Calm down," Stephen groans.

"We don't! You have to prepare for the holidays, Stephen! It's the most important time of the year for us!" she shouts, flailing her arms around.

"Don't you think I know that? It's my farm!" Stephen snaps.

Taylor glares at him, before mumbling, "It's not your farm, it's your family's, and I care too."

Stephen looks hurt, as Taylor turns toward me.

"I'm so sorry, how rude of me! Hi, I'm Taylor!" She reaches out to shake my hand.

Julian starts to say, "This is–"

But I cut him off. "I'm Jess! Julian's new lead florist. I just came to see where the flowers were grown, and check out the famous Mistletoe Meadows I've heard so much about since moving here!"

"Ah! Wow, that makes me happy. I am head of Christmas here at Petal Patch! Very proud of what we do! I just wish others would order things when I ask so Mistletoe Meadows can continue to be the wonderful thing people around town talk about all year long." She gives Stephen major side-eye as she says it.

"Ready for our meeting?" Stephen says to Julian, gesturing inside.

"Yep," Julian says, and the two walk away toward what looks like a small office.

"Have you seen Mistletoe Meadows yet?" Taylor asks.

"I haven't! I wandered the gardens and was heading there next," I tell her.

"Great! I'll walk you over and show you a few of my favorite things!" She turns and starts heading toward the giant sign beaming Mistletoe Meadows in all capital letters.

There are reindeer statues on either side, and I will admit, to me it is incredibly odd to be in a place completely Christmas themed when it's still hot and sunny outside. It's not even truly fall yet.

Taylor shows me around, and we laugh comparing our jobs and bosses.

Honestly, from what she says, Stephen does sound grumpier than Julian. Taylor beams as she shows me all of Mistletoe Meadows. The ice skating rink, where Santa sits for the month of December, the elves' workshop, and The Claus Kitchen and Cafe.

I try to imagine all the string Christmas lights and what this place might look like in the winter, and it feels like my childhood dream, to be honest. I can see why she's so proud of it.

We head back to the massive field where they grow all the Christmas trees. I admire the view. I wouldn't admit it out loud, but I do enjoy an amazing view of nature.

I'm just too stubborn to hike around and find them.

We wrap up by sitting at the cafe as I try a few pastries with her. They are delicious, and conversation is fun and light with her.

When it's time for her to get back to work, I thank her profusely for taking the time to show me around.

"If you ever want a girl's night out, text me!" I say after putting my phone number in her phone. "I think you'd love my friends, Lindsey and Brooke! Lindsey owns Rose Point Books!"

"Oh my gosh, yes! I love Lindsey, it's hard to get her out of her shell though!" She laughs.

"Not when I'm around, you'll love it!" I laugh.

I give her a hug, because it feels like I made a new friend today, and I love friendship.

I walk back up the hill toward my car.

Julian is standing by the gate waiting for me.

Chapter Sixteen

JULIAN

I DON'T KNOW WHY I'm waiting for Jess.

Yet, as soon as she comes into view, I don't regret waiting for her.

Not for a second, because she is gorgeous, even after walking around in the heat. She pulled her hair back and breathes heavily, walking up the hill.

When she glances up and makes eye contact with me, I'm immediately transported back to our night together. Sweat glistening on her forehead, looking up at me with a coy smile, as she took my cock deep in her mouth.

I shake my head to snap myself out of it.

I need to stop thinking about Jess like that. We can't have that ever again. She's my employee.

"Aw, are you waiting for me?" she asks smugly.

"No, well, technically yes. But I just got out of my meeting, and saw you coming," I lie.

"Sure." She winks at me.

"What are your plans for the rest of your day off?" I ask.

"Uh, I'm going to celebrate a friend's engagement tonight," she mumbles.

My stomach plummets.

I am also tentatively supposed to attend an engagement party tonight, although I was planning on using Jules throwing up yesterday as an excuse not to go . . .

"Brooke and Lucas?" I ask.

"Uh, yeah, how did you know?" she questions.

"I . . . uh . . . I'm supposed to go too. Lucas and I have been friends for a while," I mumble.

"Well, how about that? See you there, sailor!" she says with a salute, as she steps around me and climbs into her Jeep.

I'm back at the office on the phone with my mom.

"I wasn't going to go anymore, Mom. It's not a big deal. Jules threw up yesterday," I groan.

"Julian, Lucas has been a good friend to you. He's one of my favorites. You will celebrate him in this important moment of his life," she snaps at me.

"I will go for one hour, and then I will be home for Jules," I say.

"You will go out for as long as you need. Jules and I have a girls' night already planned. There will be frosted sugar cookies waiting for you when you get home, because Jules will be asleep by then," she states. There is no arguing with this woman.

Although, in her defense, she's let me pour every piece of myself into Jules and this shop for the past five years. She never asked me to go out, or made me try and move on previously.

I think she knows that maybe it's time, probably mother's intuition. My gut sinks at the feeling, knowing Jules won't have that in the future.

Hours later, I leave the house. I give Jules the biggest hug and tell her I love her more than anything in the world. She smiles and says, "I know."

I hop in an Uber and head down to the bar. The whole drive I fidget with my wristwatch. Nerves get the best of me. My stomach does somersaults.

I can't tell if I'm nervous because I'm leaving Jules, seeing Jess, or just going out to a bar again. Maybe it's all of the above.

We pull up, and I thank my Uber driver, heading into the bar.

As soon as I walk in, my eyes immediately find Jess.

She's talking to a guy and throws her head back in laughter.

It's the same laughter that reeled me in the first time I saw her, carefree and confident. It's captivating. She turns her head, and her eyes find mine.

She smiles at me, and all the nerves vanish.

She's sexy, and beautiful. Her hair is half up, cascading down her back in loose waves. She's wearing a skin-tight red dress that has a heart cutout in the chest. She has on black sparkly heels, accentuating her toned, tan legs.

The sight of her sends an unwanted wave of heat down my spine. I work double-time to push all those feelings deep down.

I cannot, and will not, acknowledge the way Jess makes me feel.

David walks over, slapping me on the shoulder.

"Dude, I am so happy to see you. It's awesome to see you out again. I know Lucas is going to be so happy you're here to celebrate with us." He starts guiding me over toward Lucas.

Jess gives me a little wave, and then turns to keep talking to the guy. I've never been a jealous man, but I immediately feel jealous that he gets to look at her, and I don't.

We walk over to Lucas and Brooke. I've only met Brooke once in the shop. I've been hiding for the last five years, and they only started dating three years ago.

I introduce myself to Brooke again, as Lucas smiles wide, shouting about how happy he is to see me.

David and my mom were right; he genuinely seems really happy I'm here tonight.

I'm glad I made it here for him, especially after all the support all of my friends have given me over the past five years.

Grief is a funny thing; sometimes it slaps you in the face. Sometimes it pulls you under completely. Right now, it's an all-consuming guilt that I haven't been there for these people.

I hope they never understand it either, the way I've felt. I wouldn't wish the grief I've experienced on my worst enemy. I hope Jules never knows it.

I chat with Lucas for a few minutes, catching up on his life. Eventually, Jess comes over and hugs Brooke. They start laughing about something. I'm really trying to be present with David and Lucas, but my ears keep ending up trying to listen to Jess.

"Lindsey said you went home with a guy at the bar that night! Tell me everything!" Brooke squeals.

"Oh, it was amazing, mind-blowing actually, but I won't be seeing him anymore," Jess says somberly.

"What? Mind-blowing? You have to see him again!" Brooke shouts.

"It's complicated, babe, I want to, but there are just . . . things . . . that wouldn't work now," she says softly.

"I still think you should try, you don't just let mind-blowing get away!" Brooke says with a laugh.

Lindsey walks up on the other side of Jess. "What's mind-blowing?" she asks.

"Jess said the guy she was with the other night was mind-blowing, and she doesn't even want to try and see him again!" Brooke explains.

Lindsey adds, "Yeah, well, she might be right. I don't think it would work out for them."

Later in the evening, I'm sitting in a booth nursing a whiskey Coke with David and Lucas. Brooke comes up and asks Lucas to come meet a friend of hers.

David leans over the table. "We are seriously so happy you made it tonight, man. We know it's been hard, and we just want to help."

"I know, thanks man," I say quietly.

We sit in silence for a minute.

"I'll be right back, gotta take a leak," he laughs.

I sit in the booth, twirling my glass, watching the ice cubes.

Jess sits down across from me.

"Well, imagine seeing you here." She giggles.

I can tell she's been drinking. She's on the edge between tipsy and drunk, from what I can tell.

"Thought you didn't want to be alone with me?" I ask.

"When did I say that? I would never," she says coyly.

"Literally this morning . . . in the garden," I deadpan.

"Well, morning Jess didn't mean that," she says, and then slams the rest of her drink.

I laugh. "Okay, need another drink?" I ask.

"Nope, I'm done for the night, or else I might end up back in your bed." She winks.

I chuckle. "Not tonight, tonight Jules is at my house . . . with my mother."

"Ah, I forgot you're like, responsible." She rolls her eyes.

"What's wrong with being responsible? I happen to enjoy it," I remark.

"Nothing is wrong with it. I'm just . . . not," she laughs, "which really makes my big sister mad. She'd be mad that I'm drinking tonight."

"Does her opinion matter to you?" I ask.

"No . . . yes . . . maybe?" She rests her head on the back of the booth in defeat. "My mom died when I was little, and my big sister is all I've had . . . well, and my dad but you know, my big sister was my female role model, and she kept everything together for me. So yeah, her opinion means a lot to me."

I stare at her a minute, my stomach somersaulting at the fact that her big sister kept things together for her, and Jules doesn't have that. She just has me . . .

I'm at a loss for words, but I know I need to say something. "I'm so sorry for your loss," I mumble.

"Oh, Julian, it's fine. I never felt like I was missing something on a day-to-day basis. Sarah and my dad were always more than enough, and we did so much together. It was really only the random moments throughout life where everyone else has their mom that I felt that grief resurface. I was so young when she died, so my grief was different than my dad and Sarah's. That sounds shitty . . . I don't think I'm making sense. Anyways, Sarah has always been there . . ." She chokes out that last part, but quickly composes herself. As if she isn't allowed to show her emotion, or wear her heart on her sleeve.

"There is no guidebook on grief. You're allowed to feel however you feel, Jess." I reach out instinctively and rest my hand on top of hers.

I tell myself I would do that for any woman who just told me what Jess did.

David walks back over, and I remove my hand from Jess. She smiles, and David sits down on the other side of Jess.

David and Jess start chatting about superficial things: the weather and some reality show they apparently both watch.

I'm lost in my thoughts, though, wondering if Jules will say I'm enough someday. She doesn't have a sister like Jess does, but the possibility that I'm enough fills me with hope.

Chapter Seventeen

Jess

I WAKE UP TO my phone ringing.

I'm groggy. What time is it?

I don't even know, I don't care, this is my second day off, and I have to go back to work tomorrow. I'm sleeping as much as I want.

Phyllis shouts through the wall, "Wake up and answer your phone!"

I groan and roll over, picking up my phone, to see Sarah's face staring back at me. I press answer.

"Hello?" I grumble.

"Dear god, Jess, it's almost ten. Why are you still asleep?" Sarah shouts.

"Good morning to you, too," I mumble.

"Do I need to call you later?" Sarah asks.

"Nope, I'm good, what's up?" I ask.

"Nothing, just wanted to check in, see how the new job is. Do you like your new life? I miss you," Sarah says softly.

"I miss you too, but it's only been a little over a week, Sarah," I reply.

"I know, but I miss you, kid. I've never gone a whole week without you. Just keep me updated, what's new?" she asks.

"I went to Lucas and Brooke's engagement party last night, explored the farm where the flowers for the shop are grown, made a new friend, and Lindsey meal prepped a bunch of dinners for me." I laugh. "I'm doing okay!"

Sarah laughs. "New friend? Is it a boy?" she teases.

"No, it was a girl who works at the farm, in the Mistletoe Meadows area. Which, by the way, seems amazing! You and Ethan should come up and bring Dad at Christmas!" I say.

"That sounds fun, count us in! I'll let Dad know at dinner tomorrow night. Any chance you are coming?" she asks.

"Not this week, I have to work, but I'll have a Monday off soon." I sigh.

"No problem, I can handle Dad alone, but he will miss you . . . so will I!" she says.

"I know, I miss you guys too. How are things with you guys?" I ask.

"Good! Business is going well, and Ethan is super into it. Making all kinds of TikTok videos of latte art, it's hilarious. Carol, well, she found out the 'TikTac' isn't as easy as she imagined, so she won't be leaving me to be an influencer anytime soon." Sarah laughs.

"Oh, Carol." I laugh. "Tell everyone hi for me!"

"I will, love you, Jess, glad it's going well! I'm here if you need me!" she says quietly.

"Thanks Sarah, love you too!" I reply before hanging up.

"Your sister babies you too much!" Phyllis shouts through the wall.

"Shut up, Phyllis!" I shout back.

I roll over and stare at the wall.

I think about sitting in the booth with Julian last night. He asked me what was wrong with being responsible.

I roll back over and stare at the ceiling.

What *is* wrong with being responsible?

I wouldn't consider myself irresponsible, per se, I just haven't really felt the need to be more. I've been happy with the places life has taken me.

When it comes to men, though, I've never even thought about something serious. I think I'm scared of getting hurt, or ending up alone.

My phone rings again, and Phyllis starts shouting again, "Dear god, child. I don't understand why this many people want to speak to you!"

"It's called being a fun person, Phyllis. You should try it sometime!" I shout back.

It's Lindsey, so I answer with a, "Hi!"

"Hey! You left your wallet in my purse last night," Lindsey explains.

"Ah, shit. I forgot I asked you to hold it," I groan.

"I'll be at the bookstore till seven tonight, so you are welcome to walk over and grab it. If not, I can maybe come by tonight? Oh shoot, I gotta go, an employee is asking for me. Love you, text me!" she says quickly before hanging up.

I lay there in the silence. Lindsey is a great friend. I should just walk over and get it. I'm sure the last thing she wants to do after working a long shift is walk to my place to give me my wallet. However, she totally would. She's too good to me.

I get up and start getting ready.

I make it to Rose Point Books, and I'm irritated because I couldn't even stop for a tea at the coffee shop without my wallet.

As soon as I step through the door, though, I'm instantly in a better mood. It smells like books and pumpkin spice in here.

Lindsey stocks up on pumpkin spice candles for the entire year every fall, so it always smells delicious here.

She always brushes off this shop when people compliment her, saying it was her grandma's and all she did was take over. But she's done so much more. She brought this place to life. I once watched her add 500 crystals to a chandelier by hand to hang from the ceiling. This place is all Lindsey now, and I wish she would give herself more credit.

People come in regularly to take pictures at the gorgeous photo backdrops she has installed, or to hang out at the tables and chairs working. There are a few people who work remotely from here almost every day just because they love the environment she created.

And she made that, not her grandma.

Lindsey chats with a customer in the romance section, which is her favorite. I walk up and down the aisles pretending to look through the books. I'm not much of a reader, unlike Lindsey and my sister. I'd rather waste my life watching shitty reality television.

She finishes up with the customer and walks over.

"Hi!" she whispers.

"Do I need to be quiet? Is this a library?" I ask.

She laughs. "No, I just try to respect the people working."

"Ah, gotcha!" I mumble softly.

"I'll go grab your wallet from the back, be right back!" She waves while walking off.

I look at my phone and scroll through my Instagram feed. The front door chime goes off, and I hear a squeal. "Jess!"

I bring my phone down just in time to be barrelled into by Jules.

"Oh well, hey there, bug!" I boop her nose.

"Bug? I'm not a bug?" she scowls.

I laugh. "No of course not, you're beautiful. Sorry, my sister called me bug when I was little, and I always liked it. Even though I think she secretly meant it in a rude way. May have started out because I *bug* her."

"Oh, that's a funny story. I guess you can call me bug!" She squeezes me in a tight hug.

I look up to find Julian staring at us.

"Hey," he whispers.

"Hi," I reply.

Lindsey comes back out with my wallet, handing it to me.

"Thanks! This is Jules, and you remember Julian, my boss," I tell her, gesturing toward them.

"Jess, is this your sister?" Jules asks.

"Aw," I laugh. "No, but she might as well be. She's my best friend."

"I wish I had a best friend," Jules whines.

I crouch down, so I'm eye level with Jules. "You will someday, bug. It took me a long time to find her. But for now, I can be your best friend too."

I smile up at Lindsey.

Lindsey clasps her hands together. "So, can I help you guys find anything?" she asks Julian.

"Uh, yes, actually. We are here to pick up the first grade book for the school book study?" he tells Lindsey.

"Oh, perfect, there is a shelf right over there with all the school books on it." She smiles at Julian, gesturing toward the small kids section.

"Great, thanks! Jujubee, let's go find it?" he says to Jules.

"No! I want to spend time with Jess!" she shouts.

"Shh! Jules, we have to be quiet here," Julian says patiently.

"Jess!" Jules whines.

"He's right, bug. We have to be quiet for all the nice people working. Let's go find your book." I grab her hand, and squeeze it. I direct her over to the shelf Lindsey pointed at.

When we get to the shelf it says "Rose Point Schools" across the top. Each shelf is labeled with a school, and I'm guessing the books are in order by grade-level?

"Hmm, you're in high school, right?" I ask Jules.

"No, silly!" she squeals, "I'm in first grade!"

"Oh that's right, sorry, you're just such a beautiful, mature, young lady, I forgot," I whisper.

She smiles up at me.

I look at her for a second and realize I want this. I want a little girl. I want a life with someone, where we have kids and a house with a yard.

I shake my head and get a grip on my heart, telling myself I'm not even close to ready for those things.

She points at the second book on the shelf. "That's it! That's the one Mrs. Garcia showed us!" She smiles. She's still squeezing my hand, and my heart squeezes a little with it.

I grab the book off the shelf, and pull it down.

"Oh, *Charlotte's Web*! It's one of my favorites!" I hand it to her.

"Really?" she asks excitedly.

"Yep, when you're done reading it, we should watch the movie!" I tell her.

"You want to watch a movie with me?" She jumps up and down.

I laugh. "Who wouldn't want to? You're the best! I'll bring the popcorn."

She grins.

"Dad, did you hear that? Jess said there is a movie!" she squeals, finally letting go of my hand and running over to Julian.

"I heard," he says softly. I can't quite read the expression on his face, whether he is upset with me or angry. He definitely is not happy, though.

"Well, friends, I have to head out. More errands to run before I go back to work tomorrow!" I wave at them.

"No! Don't go yet!" Jules cries.

"I'll see you again soon, bug! Don't forget we have a movie date!" I wink at her.

"Okay," she whines.

I grab her hand and twirl her around before giving her a hug.

"Be good for your dad, okay?" I whisper.

"I will." She giggles.

"See you tomorrow?" I question Julian.

"Yeah, see you then," he says quietly.

I walk back over to Lindsey, who just finished helping another woman in the romance section.

"Alright, I'm out of here. See you soon, right?" I ask.

"Yep! You can't go more than two days without seeing me now that you live here," she laughs.

I laugh too. "Love you bunches!"

"Oh, wait, Jess!" she shouts.

I turn around.

She walks over and gets close before whispering, "Be careful," in a serious tone.

"Of what?" I ask.

"Of him." She nods her head toward Julian. "The way he looks at you doesn't scream *that's my employee.*"

"Lindsey, you're crazy." I chuckle.

"No, I'm an unbiased third party who reads and writes romance in my free time. I know that look. It's the look of love," she scolds.

"Oh my gosh, no. Bye, Linds, see you later." I laugh my way out the door.

She's delusional. Julian looks at me like an annoying problem he can't wait to get rid of. The look of love happened on our first night together, or so I thought. Although I'm trying to completely forget that night alto-gether.

Chapter Eighteen

JULIAN

THE SHOP SMELLS LIKE roses and chaos. There are petals scattered all over the floor, and vases everywhere. A tower of empty cardboard boxes teeters in the corner like a game of Jenga no one asked to play.

I'm stressed. I had to close early because the shop's ancient point-of-sale system broke down again, and I'm currently trying to set up a new one.

Jess bursts through the back door, holding an armful of tangled eucalyptus like it's a trophy.

"Okay, hear me out: eucalyptus jungle arch. For the Smith wedding. We lean into a full Tarzan fantasy. I think they will love it," Jess squeals.

"That sounds like a nightmare to assemble," I grumble.

"Nightmares can be *beautiful,* Julian. Like that one I had where I was chased by sentient tulips. Honestly? Gorgeous. No notes," Jess says.

"Do you ever stop talking?" I groan. Honestly, I'm not in the mood, and I need to start being harsh with Jess. I don't want her to get the wrong idea.

"Do you ever start smiling?" she chirps.

She dumps the eucalyptus out onto the counter in front of me. A stray sprig bounces up and hits me in the face. I close my eyes, and take a deep breath.

"You know this is a business right? A flower shop? This isn't a playground," I snap.

"Flowers are nature's playground. I'm just their hype woman." She shrugs.

"Well, nature needs you to stop rearranging the display table every morning. I put those sunflowers there for a reason," I say.

"Yeah. And that reason was *boring,*" she sings, and grins at me. "I added whimsy. You're welcome." She bows.

I finally look her in the eyes. It's electric, and I blink away quickly.

"Whimsy doesn't pay the bills," I mumble.

"Neither does boring, and yet here you are," she says smugly.

She leans closer to me, glancing at the point-of-sale system, and then looking at me. It's a little too close, and I notice. She smirks, like she notices me noticing.

"You're impossible." I sigh.

"And yet, you haven't fired me. I've made it over a full week." She smiles.

There is a pause, while I look at her, really look at her. She's gorgeous like always, wearing a black sweater with a black and white skirt. They hug all the curves that I remember all too well. I wish I could forget the feeling of them from our night together.

"God knows why," I mumble.

She leans in a little bit more, resting her elbows on the counter.

"Maybe because you *like* me." She bats her eyes at me.

"Maybe because you're the only person who can keep the dahlias alive," I say assertively.

"Uh-huh. And maybe because you watched me for *a full ten seconds* when I danced with that bouquet earlier today," she whispers.

"You were shaking maracas made out of roses," I snap.

"It was inspired," she sings.

"It was a safety hazard," I groan.

"You care about my safety? Julian, some may consider that you like me if you're worried about my safety," she says softly.

I open my mouth, and then close it.

"Do you ever get tired?" I ask.

"Of what?" she questions.

"Of being . . . this." I gesture vaguely.

She grins like she won something.

"Never, but I think you get tired of pretending you don't like it." She smirks.

I stand there for a moment, feeling caught. She's right; I love her confidence, the way she captures my attention in every way.

"Go restack those boxes before they kill someone," I grumble.

Copying my gruff tone, Jess mocks me, "Go restack the boxes!" She gets the flirty edge to her voice again. "Say it nicer and I'll think about it."

"Go restack the boxes . . . please," I say.

I make sure to say it sensually, and she looks shocked for a minute, that I engaged in her flirty behavior.

She regains her composure, winks, and saunters off, the eucalyptus trailing behind her like a wedding veil. I fight a smile, and think to myself, *I'm so screwed*.

Later that afternoon, Jess and I work hard to complete the rearranging she suggested for the store. I hate to admit it, but as soon as we finally finish, it looks amazing.

"You love it, don't you?" She smirks.

"I hate to admit it, but yeah. It looks good," I tell her.

She pauses a moment, looking around with pride, before saying, "How did you envision the store when you opened it?"

A lump forms in my throat.

"I didn't," I whisper.

"You didn't imagine what it would look like?" she questions.

"I . . . No, Hannah did. This was Hannah's store, I just had to take over, after . . ." I say softly. I can't bring myself to speak the words out loud.

"Oh, I should've . . . I'm sorry," Jess says quietly.

Jess reaches over and gives my hand a squeeze, with a weak smile.

For a brief moment, my heart flutters before the front door chimes.

Jess turns and walks to the front, before I hear her shout, "Oh my god! Hi!"

I look toward the front and see her hugging Brooke aggressively.

"What are you doing here?" Jess asks her.

"Well, it's time to start wedding planning. I figured I could start with the easiest thing– a florist. Because obviously it's you. I can't have anyone else do the flowers for my wedding!" she exclaims.

Jess looks beautiful smiling at her friend. She looks proud of her friend, but also slightly proud of herself. Jess radiates confidence, in the best way. It's part of what makes her absolutely stunning.

"Brooke! I am so excited! This will be amazing! Come sit with me at the consultation counter. We can go over colors, pricing, and figure out what you're thinking!" Jess squeals.

Jess loves this job. It's easy to see, and everyone can tell. Watching her light up at the idea of wedding flowers brings a smile to my face.

Brooke waves hi to me as her and Jess head to the consultation counter. I wave back before going to the register to get some more work done.

Chapter Nineteen

JESS

I'M TRYING REALLY HARD to focus on Brooke and her wedding after Julian dropped the bomb that this shop wasn't actually his, but his late wife's.

It's hard for me to imagine with how much love and care he puts into this place that it hasn't always been his.

At the same time, I know my dad would've done the same thing had my mom had something special like this that she left behind. My dad has worked hard to keep everything my mom ever loved in near-perfect condition.

I respect Julian for putting so much effort into this store, even though it wasn't something he personally wanted.

Hannah must've been someone truly special, and I wonder if I'll ever find that kind of love. The kind my parents had.

Brooke tells me that they are going to try and get married two months from today, and I'm a little shocked at the rapidness of it.

I lean close and whisper, "Are you pregnant?"

She starts laughing loudly. "Gosh, no. Just happy and excited, and why wait? I don't need a big, fancy wedding. I just need Lucas."

"Okay! I just had to ask, because I cannot imagine wanting to rush into a wedding." I chuckle.

"Someday you will understand. Or maybe you won't, maybe you'll want some big fancy wedding," she says.

"Nah, I'll probably elope in a casino or something. I feel like that's probably more me." I laugh, even though it stings a little.

Brooke reaches over and grabs my hand. "You'll find someone who loves you for you. You'll find someone who you don't have to pretend around. Who you don't need to put on your hot mess act for. Someone who you can take your makeup off in front of. I know you will." She squeezes my hand.

My eyes water slightly before I bat her hand away, "Girl, I don't need a man, you know that."

She laughs. "I know you better than you think I do."

"Yeah, yeah, so anyways . . . flowers." I start flipping through our wedding floral inspiration albums, getting a feel for what she wants so we can plan this wedding.

While we look through the photos, I look over at Julian, and he's looking at me. We lock eyes for a minute, and butterflies erupt in my stomach.

Butterflies I try to shoo away, because I can't have feelings for this man.

Later that night, Lindsey and I hang out at her place. Lindsey's place is the best. It's the coziest, most comfortable home above her bookstore. Her building is actually three stories. She's kept so many of the gorgeous historic elements the building has. She's also kept a lot of her grandmother's furniture and decor, but brought fresh new life to them.

Her whole place screams cottagecore. It should be in one of those home living magazines, honestly.

Lindsey cooks while I play fetch with Scout.

I convinced Lindsey to cook pasta tonight, and not some healthy chicken crap. It smells delicious, and I cannot wait to eat. My stomach is growling.

"Is it done yet?" I whine.

Lindsey rolls her eyes. "Yes, child, it's almost done. Can you feed Scout?"

"Yeah, no problem," I answer.

I feed Scout, and then head to the kitchen.

"Can I help with anything?" I ask.

"Yeah, you can cut up the garlic bread there." She points to the bread on her island.

"Okay," I respond. I wait a minute before asking, "How's the bookstore? Is business good?"

"Yeah, it's actually going really well. Partnering with all the schools helped offset all the slow summer sales. I feel like I can breathe again and not worry about whether I'd be able to pay the extra staff I hired in the spring. How's the flower shop?" she asks.

"Good, we finally finished the last of the rearranging. I personally think it looks amazing. I'm hopeful it will only help Julian's business. The B.Y.O.Bouquet already seems to be a huge hit," I tell her.

"I'm surprised Julian's letting you move everything around in his store. I'd have a hard time if I hired someone who wanted to change everything." Lindsey laughs.

"Well, turns out it wasn't his store . . ." I whisper.

"What?" Lindsey shouts.

"It was Hannah's . . . his wife's?" I explain.

"Wow." Lindsey sighs. "That's hard."

"Yeah," I whisper.

"Well, it's good for you I guess . . . you can do what you've always wanted to do, and run that flower shop like it's your own," she says with a smile.

"Yeah, I guess so," I whisper.

But I feel a little guilty at the thought of that.

I worked all day today with Becky. Julian had the day off, although he still came in with Jules for a little bit in the morning.

I chatted with her about her love for Princess Elsa, to which I explained that Elsa is a terrible sister, and she should pick a new favorite princess.

Julian scowled at me and told me, "She can like whatever princess she wants."

Agree to disagree. No child of mine will ever idolize a horrible sister.

I'm crazy tired by the time I make it to my apartment that night. I lay on my bed watching *Love Island* again, until I fall asleep.

I wake up abruptly to another phone call. Why are people always calling me while I'm sleeping? Sarah would tell me it's because I spend too much of my life sleeping.

I roll over and see the clock, five a.m. Who calls this early?

It's the number I have saved as Julian.

I answer quickly. "Hello?" I say, trying not to sound groggy.

"Uh, hi, Jess, could you . . . uhm . . . listen, I know you said you'd babysit, I'm not sure if you were serious, but uh . . . I need help," he says nervously.

"Julian, spit it out. What do you need?" I say firmly.

"My mom is in the hospital. I need to go down there, but I don't know how bad the situation is yet. I'm not ready to take Jules down there until I know what's going on. Could you come hang out with her this morning?" he asks.

"I'll be there as fast as I can," I say before hanging up.

I leap out of bed and throw a pair of sweatpants on. I toss my hair in a bun, and start frantically grabbing my stuff.

Phyllis shouts through the wall, "Who on earth would ask you to babysit? Horrid idea. You should never be left alone with a child, you're a child yourself!"

"Not now, Phyllis!" I shout as I run out the door.

Luckily, I remember where Julian lives. I try really hard not to think about our night together as he answers the door. He answers the door in gray sweatpants, though, so all the images of the night come flooding back. I try not to look at his dick, but fail slightly as my eyes fall downward.

He pretends he doesn't notice, but his cheeks turn a shade of pink.

"She should sleep a little while longer, when she wakes up just tell her I had to go help her grandma. I'll call and let you know when I'll be back," he whispers, grabbing his keys.

"No problem, don't worry. We'll have fun," I whisper back with a smile.

"Yeah, that's what I'm worried about . . ." he whispers.

"Julian, seriously, I'll take good care of her. Check on your mom, and keep me updated," I say softly.

A small tear forms in his left eye, but he blinks it away. "Thanks. I would've asked Becky, but she works the morning shift, and I knew you were late shift."

"You don't need to explain. I'm happy to help. I love that little girl. Now go, keep me posted," I whisper.

"Thanks, Jess," he says, and then turns and runs out. I close the door and lock it behind him.

I turn around and look around his house. It's exactly as I remembered, and of course now that I'm looking at it with new information, I should've known a woman lived here at some point. I walk down the hall to the closed door. I carefully and quietly peek in.

Jules sleeps in her pink room, snuggling with a stuffed hippo. She looks so sweet and peaceful.

I walk back down the hall to the living room and cuddle up on the couch. I doubt I'll fall back asleep, but I'll take whatever rest I can get before that cute little monster wakes up.

Chapter Twenty

JULIAN

Why did I call Jess?

I feel like I keep making these wild decisions when it comes to Jess, and I cannot figure out why.

I needed help, and I hate asking for help.

Why did I wait for her at Petal Patch Acres the other day? Why did I call her this morning? Why did I just leave my kid with her? Why do I look for her at work? Why do I wonder what her favorite food is?

My mind spirals on my drive to the hospital.

Even crazier, why am I thinking about her right now instead of my mom?

Probably because thinking of my mom makes me sick to my stomach right now. If something happens to her, I don't think I can handle it.

I don't think I'm mentally strong enough right now. Jules doesn't deserve to lose anyone else, and I'm so damn scared of losing anyone else.

I try to force myself not to think of Jess most days, but this morning, as I make this horrible drive, I let myself think about Jess, because the alternative thoughts are worse.

I didn't expect to ever have feelings again. I thought I buried all my feelings with Hannah. After she died, I really thought that part of me had gone with her—like love had been carved out of me and buried alongside her. And for a while, it had. The years passed, and the house didn't echo with her laughter anymore, just with memories too loud to ignore.

But now ... there's Jess, and it's nothing like it was with Hannah. But it's not nothing either. Jess makes me laugh again, without trying. She looks at me like I'm not broken, and I constantly find myself wanting to share stupid things, to just ... hear her voice. And then the guilt crashes into me like a wave.

Is this betrayal? Or is this healing? I swore I'd never forget Hannah. I haven't. I won't. Her face still comes to me in dreams. Her voice is still the one I hear when I need courage. But does loving someone new mean I loved her less? Or does it mean I learned from her how to love better?

God, she would've smiled at this. She was always the one telling me I had too much heart to let it wither away. She'd want me to live. I know that; we even talked about it while she was still here. About finding that passion, but knowing it doesn't make it easier.

I'm just scared. Scared to open the door again. Scared that I'm not allowed to feel joy without Hannah in the picture, but maybe that's not true. Maybe I can carry her with me, without keeping myself locked in the past.

Maybe this love doesn't replace, it adds. Maybe there's room for someone new, without erasing the woman who made me who I am.

I push it all down, parking my car at the hospital and running in as fast I can.

I step into the hospital, and it all comes flooding back. It's bright, busy, and too sterile. The hum of fluorescent lights and the scent of disinfectant flood my senses.

I stand at the doors, afraid to move, when a nurse comes up. "Can I help you?"

"Uh, yes, I'm looking for my mother . . ." I say quietly, and I give her my mom's info.

"Wait here one moment. I'll find out where she is for you." The nurse smiles politely at me before walking away.

The nausea of nerves threatens to have me heading to a bathroom any second. Hannah died here in this hospital, and I haven't been back since.

The nurse finally makes her way back. "I'll take you to her, right this way." She gestures to a hall on the left, and I follow numbly.

Trying to block out all the feelings.

She gestures to a door. "Right in here, let me know if you need anything." She quickly walks away.

I grab the handle and take a deep breath.

The room is modest, clean, with a small window letting in a pale wash of the light from the sunrise. Mom's eyes are closed, but her chest moves up and down.

A nurse is adjusting the IV bag when I walk in and gives me a small wave. "You must be Julian," she whispers. "Your mom has been talking about you with every single nurse here."

"Oh god," I mumble quietly.

She laughs softly. "Your mom is doing okay! I'm happy to inform you that the lab work shows it's just a UTI. Which can be pretty rough and scary for our older patients, but she'll be fine. Probably out of here later this morning."

"Thank you so much," I whisper.

There is a flood of relief that washes over me as the nurse exits the room. I walk over and start poorly adjusting my mom's blanket.

She opens her eyes, sits up in bed, looking a little tired but amused. "Julian, you're tucking that blanket in like it insulted your manhood," she mumbles.

"It's crooked. You deserve a symmetrical recovery," I whisper, and give her a smile. I reach for her hand and give it a tight squeeze.

She smiles up at me. "I've survived worse things, like your haircut in high school, and that awful school play you did in the sixth grade."

I chuckle, and sink into the chair next to her. The heaviness of everything hits me then. I glance out the window, blinking to stop any tears from falling.

She squeezes my hand. "Julian, look at me." I glance at her. "How bad was it walking in here?" she asks softly.

"It hit me like a punch to the face," I whisper. "It's the same corridor, same elevator ding, and same antiseptic smell. I thought I was gonna throw up."

"Oh, honey . . ." Mom whispers.

"I keep thinking about how Hannah smiled at me right before they took her into surgery. I didn't know it would be the last smile. I didn't *know*, Mom." My voice cracks as I let a few tears trickle down my face.

"No one ever does, sweetie," she says.

There is a long moment of silence between us.

"I haven't been back here in five years, I haven't . . . I couldn't. I wanted to bring flowers and cards to the nurses like Hannah wanted. I couldn't though. It felt like if I walked these halls again, I'd find pieces of her. Or worse, pieces of me I don't want back," I admit. "I could've come back; it's been five years."

Mom squeezes my hand again.

"Grief does that. It tells you that if you stay still, you'll stay safe. But honey, you've been standing in one spot for too long," she explains.

"Mom, I–I messed up." It comes out before I can stop the words from happening. Like I need to tell someone. "I, that night you had a sleepover with Jules. I met Jess, before I knew she was my employee and we . . ." I can't tell my mom that part. "I had feelings, I didn't think I'd ever have feelings again. I kicked her out in the morning, and then she showed up at Blossom Bliss. It's been hell. I can't like her. For a million reasons, I can't like her."

"Oh, but that girl . . . I like that girl for you." My mom smiles. "And she definitely likes you."

"I kind of figured when she showed up disheveled to watch Jules this morning . . ." I whisper-laugh.

"You asked her to watch Jules?" my mom asks, surprised.

"Yeah, who else would?" I ask.

"Well, a lot of people *would*, you just don't let them. I think you know how you feel based on the fact she's currently alone with your little girl." She smiles.

"Mom, she doesn't know half of what she's dealing with," I explain.

"Just be honest with her, Julian. Quit hiding from your happiness," she says softly.

"What if I'm still broken?" I finally ask.

"Then let her see the cracks. That's where the light gets in," she says.

I swallow, fighting all my emotions.

"I'm scared, Mom," I whisper.

"Good, that means you're alive again." She laughs sadly. There is a long pause before she says, "I don't want this place to haunt you anymore. I want it to be just another building. With horrible food and terrible lighting."

"The lighting is terrible, huh?" I laugh, looking up at the sterile fluorescent panels overhead. "You're very zen for someone hooked up to an IV."

"Morphine is basically enlightenment in liquid form." She chuckles.

We share a long look, before I let go of her hand, and rest my head back on the headrest.

"Julian . . . Don't wait for grief to let go of you. You have to let go of it," she whispers, as she closes her eyes too.

I stare at the wall, and feel a small sense of relief. It felt good to share my feelings with someone.

Chapter Twenty-One

JESS

I HEAR THE PITTER-PATTER of tiny feet coming down the hall.

"Jules?" I whisper.

She peeks around the corner.

"Jess? What are you doing here?" she whispers as she rubs her eyes and yawns.

"Oh, you know, I just wanted to see my favorite girl at seven in the morning!" I say with a smile.

"Where's my dad? Are you and my dad in love?" she asks.

"Oh, uh, no, uh, your dad had to go help your grandma this morning, and asked me to come hang out with you for a little bit," I answer.

"Is Grandma okay?" she asks nervously.

"Oh yeah, don't worry bug!" I say with a big smile. I haven't heard from Julian, but I hope I'm right that they don't need to worry. Both Jules and Julian have gone through enough. "Now, how about some breakfast?" I ask her.

"Okay!" she says, jumping up and down.

I make my way into the kitchen and open the cabinet, and find no cereal . . .

"So, uh, do you not eat cereal?" I question.

"Dad says it isn't good for me, too much sugar for the morning," she grumbles.

"Bah humbug. Your dad's wrong. I'll get you some cereal later today, how about . . . for now, we go get some pancakes?" I ask.

Her eyes go wide. "Are you serious?"

"Yeah, why? Do you not like pancakes?" I ask.

"I love pancakes!" she shouts.

"Great, how fast can you get dressed and out the door?" I ask her.

"Give me five minutes!" she squeals, running down the hall.

"I'll be here!" I shout.

I get a text from Julian:

> She's okay, she'll need to stay here for a little while, but I'll be home soon. I can bring Jules back here with me.

> No rush! Jules and I are going to have breakfast, she just woke up a few minutes ago. Take your time :)

> Thank you Jess, seriously.

> No problem :)

I put my phone away, as Jules comes out in sweatpants and a *KPOP Demon Hunters* shirt. "Can you make my hair look like yours?" she asks.

I reach up and touch the bun on top of my head. I completely forgot that I'm in basically pajamas with no makeup on. I can't go out like this.

"I can make your hair much prettier than mine!" I laugh.

"No, I want to look just like you! You're the prettiest!" she cries.

My heart melts. I walk over and kneel down to her level. "No, you are the prettiest girl in the whole wide world. Exactly how you are. But no problem, I'll put your hair up like mine. Do you have a hair tie?"

She runs off toward the bathroom, coming back with a hair tie and her stuffed hippo. I take the hair tie, and start putting her hair up in a bun. "And who is this handsome young fellow?" I ask, gesturing to the hippo.

"This is Professor Peanut Pickle Poppypants!" she yells.

"Oh. Wow, a professor! I'm honored to make his acquaintance." I bow my head.

I finish making her bun, and she runs over to the mirror. "I love it, I look just like you!" she squeals with delight.

"Ready for some pancakes?" I ask her with a smile.

"Eek! I'm ready!" She jumps up and down.

And for the first time in forever, I'm going to go out in public in sweatpants with no makeup on. With not even a little bit of lipstick in sight. Because I promised the cutest girl in the world pancakes, and I'm not going to let my own insecurities stop me from getting them for her.

We had so much fun at breakfast. We both got chocolate chip pancakes with a smiley face made out of whipped cream and cherries on top.

We colored our kids' menus, and talked about her school. I asked her what her favorite thing to do was, and she said paint, play Barbies, and going to work with her dad.

I brought her back home, and we painted pictures of flowers. Now we are making friendship bracelets together while listening to Taylor Swift.

Jules said she doesn't know Taylor Swift super well because her dad listens to "old people music."

I make her a little bracelet that says "Lil Bestie." When I hand it to her she asks me what a bestie is and I explain, it's just like a "best friend."

She smiles at me. "I've never had a best friend before!"

"Well, now you do. I told you the other day at the bookstore I'd be yours!" I boop her little nose, and she giggles.

"Is this what it's like?" Jules whispers.

"What sweetie?" I ask.

"Having a mom?" she says sadly, her little eyes dropping down like she's done something wrong.

"Oh, I . . . I don't know," I admit quietly.

She stares at me, eyes wide for a second.

"My mom died when I was little too, so I don't really remember a whole lot," I explain softly.

"Oh, well . . . it's nice to know I'm not the only one. Sometimes it feels like I'm the only kid without a mom," she says.

My heart sinks. I remember that feeling. "I know that feeling, and you'll feel that way again . . . and even though you don't remember her. You'll miss your mom, and still love her no matter what."

My eyes start to fill with tears, but I blink them away and give her little hand a squeeze.

She smiles at me. "Do you miss your mom still?"

"Yep, every day. It comes in waves, and sometimes I think I've buried it down, and won't let it bother me. But, I know it's part of who I am. It's why I live everyday like it could be my last," I admit.

I realize in this moment with Jules, that I tend to brush off my grief and the way my mom's death has impacted my life. It is, sadly, part of who I am though.

I give her a quick little hug, just because I know she probably doesn't understand everything I just said. But I know she probably needs one. I feel close to Jules just based on the fact that we ended up in similar situations in life.

"Thanks, Jess," she whispers as I release her.

A second later, Julian walks in the door, and turns to see us sitting on the floor of his living room making bracelets.

He doesn't smile. He just stares for a minute. I'm not sure what is going through his mind, but I can tell it's heavy.

"Hey," I say softly.

"Daddy!" Jules leaps off the floor, and runs over to her dad, wrapping him in a big hug. "We ate smiley face pancakes, painted flowers, and made bracelets!" She holds her tiny wrist up for him to examine.

"Wow! Sounds like fun, sorry I missed it, Jujubee." He hugs her again.

He turns to me and we lock eyes for a moment, before Jules finishes her bracelet and asks me to tie it.

I tie the string, and hand it to her. "No, it's for you, silly!" She laughs.

I look down at the bracelet, that says "Best Frend" with the "i" missing.

"I love it," I whisper, and give her a big hug.

"Alright, Jules, Jess has to head to work, so can you tell her bye and thank you?" Julian interrupts.

"Aw, I don't want her to go!" Jules yells.

"I know, bug, but I'll be back. I'm like Frosty the Snowman– I'll be back again someday!" I squeeze her one more time, and head over to the door to put my shoes on.

"Jujubee, can you go grab your shoes? We are going to head out in a few . . ." Julian says to Jules.

"Ugh, fine!" Jules whines, stomping off toward her room.

I watch her walk away and then have a moment of panic, and my stomach drops. I can feel my bare skin. It's too real, and too unfiltered for Julian to see. Normally I would have spiraled by now, already reaching for a compact mirror or an excuse to slip away to the bathroom. How had I not remembered? Not noticed?

Strangely, though ... I don't feel the urge to hide like I normally do. I feel no prickling embarrassment, no frantic scramble to go fix myself. Just a warmth spreading through my chest, loosening something I didn't realize I kept closed tight. I'm not wearing makeup. And I am okay. With him, I am okay.

For once, I don't feel painted or performed. I just feel . . . myself. And it is somehow enough.

Julian turns to me, and my breath catches. I always forget just how handsome he is. His jaw defined and covered in stubble. His light blue eyes squint slightly as he looks at me. I wish I didn't know what it felt like to kiss this man, because I think it's ruined me now.

"Thank you," Julian whispers, just inches away from me. So close I can feel his breath on my lips. It instantly brings a sense of need and urgency over my body. I *need* to kiss this man. I can't though; he doesn't want it. Plus, I need this job to work out. I can't fuck this up, I've already fucked up enough of my life.

I need to be strong, but the way he is looking at me right now . . .

It doesn't feel like he doesn't want this. It feels like the opposite. It feels like he wants me, now more than ever.

Although, I've misread this man before. I thought we had something special and he easily kicked me out the next morning.

"No problem." I finally get the words out. "I was happy to help."

He takes a tiny step closer, and grabs the back of my head, like he's going to push me up against this door and kiss me.

When Jules' door slams down the hall and he takes a giant step back, shaking his head.

"Uh, bye!" I panic at the feeling of possibly being rejected, and leave.

I don't look back. I just head straight home to get ready for my shift.

Chapter Twenty-Two

JULIAN

I almost kissed Jess . . . again.

This time with my kid home, which would have been a huge mistake.

Jules and I spent the rest of yesterday with my mom at the hospital. We brought her lunch, and stayed until dinnertime.

I offered to stay for dinner too, but she insisted I go home with Jules since it was a school night. Since she is my mom, I still listen to her . . . sometimes.

I dropped Jules off at school this morning. Jess and I are working the morning shift, and Becky is coming in early so I can go check on my mom this afternoon before I have to pick up Jules from school.

I don't know what I'll do when Becky leaves because this is us with an 'extra set of hands' right now. Things are only getting busier, so I'll probably have to hire another florist.

Jess finishes up with a customer and walks over.

"What's going on in that big head of yours?" She laughs.

"Just thinking we may still need to hire another person. We are busier, and Becky is leaving soon," I explain.

"Hm, yeah. Not a bad thought. Can you afford another employee? Or can one of the others step up and work more hours?" she asks.

"If things keep going the way they have been, then yeah, absolutely. Plus we have a few more weddings than normal as well. One wedding, you and I will both be in the bridal party, so we will have to figure that out ahead of time." I laugh.

"Oh, I didn't even think about that." She laughs. "That's why you're the boss."

"No, I'm the boss because my wife died." I laugh, and then stop. Jess and I both just stare at each other.

I don't know why I said it. It isn't funny, but it felt good? It felt good to find some sense of humor about my situation. I know Hannah would've wanted this. She would love to see what this store is doing, and she would laugh that I'm the one who has been doing it all these years.

Before she passed I think we both thought I'd sell the store if she didn't make it.

Jess clears her throat. "Uhm, was that the first time you made a joke about it? 'Cause it seems like you're spiraling."

"Uh, yeah," I mumble.

"Well, dark humor is honestly pretty great for grief ..." She laughs. "The amount of times my friends complained about their moms in high school, and I'd make a joke about not having to worry about that ..."

"Yeah I guess ..." I laugh.

"Well, anyway," she mumbles. "You can always talk to me, Julian, if you need."

"Thanks Jess." I give her a weary smile. "I think I messed up. I'm sorry about that first night. I wasn't ready for what happened. Not even a little bit, and that's not to say I regret it ... it was, well it was fucking amazing." I laugh, remembering Jess swirling her tongue around . . . not now Julian. "Anyway, I wasn't ready, and that wasn't fair to you. You're amazing Jess, and you deserve the world. I can't give it to you though, but I can give you friendship and a cool place to work?"

"Friendship and a cool place to work is all I need Julian." She smiles that electric smile at me, and I wish I could take it all back. I wish I could give Jess so much more than just friendship and a cool place to work. She deserves better than me, though, and I know this is for the best.

I friend zoned Jess thirteen minutes ago, and now she is hamming it up with some idiot in a Kansas City Chiefs shirt. He looks like a douche, and when I told Jess she deserved the world I didn't mean some dipshit who came in to order flowers for his girlfriend, and is now asking Jess for her number.

To my utter shock, she gives it to him.

When he finally fucking leaves my store empty-handed, I storm over to Jess. "What the fuck was that?" I yell.

"What was what?" she asks, confused.

"That douchecanoe! Not only did you lose his business because you flirted with him, but then you're handing out your number? That's unprofessional Jess!" I shout.

Why am I so angry? I literally just told this woman I want to be friends.

"First of all, jackass, he still ordered flowers, here is the receipt. Second of all, I gave him the store number because he needs floral arrangements for a large banquet he is hosting two weeks from now," she snaps.

"Oh," I pause.

"Yeah, oh. Also, it's none of your business. You're my boss and my friend, remember?" she says sarcastically.

"Yeah," I mumble.

There is a long pause of us staring at each other, breathing heavily. Never in my life has a woman looking pissed done something to me sexually, but here I am. Getting slightly hard at the sight of her.

I glance down to the v of her neckline so briefly, and then force my eyes back to her. She doesn't miss it though.

She smirks. "Now, that I've calmed down. I have to ask . . . Were you jealous, Julian?"

"No. I was worried about your professionalism," I snap.

"Okay, good, 'cause we are friends, and you're my boss, remember?" She leans over slightly as she says it, and it takes every ounce of willpower in me not to look down again.

But I know what they feel like. God, I know what *she* feels like.

I try so fucking hard to forget, but I can't. Instead I've been jerking off more than I did as a horny teenager to the memories of that night.

Jess licks her red lips, and moves closer.

I try to think of anything other than Jess to prevent getting a full blown boner in my store right now.

I'm saved by the door chime. Jess and I move apart quickly as Becky walks in.

She spots me and says a cheery hello.

"Hey Becky, thanks for coming in early!" I tell her.

"Of course, I only have a couple weeks left, so I might as well enjoy it while I can!" she sings.

"Speaking of, can you pop into my office super quick to sign something?" I ask Becky. "Jess, will you be okay for just a sec?"

"Of course," Jess says matter-of-factly.

I head to the back with Becky.

"Are you going to tell me what that was about?" Becky asks once we step into my office.

"What?" I ask, confused.

"You guys were like making googly eyes at each other. The second I walked in you guys leaped ten miles apart like you're guilty or something." Becky laughs. "I'm not an idiot. I know the girl likes you."

I laugh. "Likes me?"

"Yeah, when you're not here she's always looking around for you. And when you are here she's always looking at you." Becky chuckles.

"Becky, it's complicated, but nothing is happening. The business is in good hands, Jess and I actually work well together. Business is better than ever; you have nothing to worry about," I reassure her.

"I'm not worried!" Becky laughs. "Be with her already!"

"What?" I shout.

"I picked her Julian. I know she's perfect for you!" she snaps.

"Becky, you picked a lead florist, this isn't some dating show. Besides, you're . . . you were one of Hannah's best friends." I get choked up at the end.

"Hannah would want me to interfere. You've done nothing but this business for five years Julian, a business you aren't even passionate about. So I brought passion and a whole lot of skill and experience to you." She smiles, a proud smile.

"I . . . Becky, I have to go. We will talk about this later. Here is the paper for you to sign, you can just leave it on my desk." I groan, handing her the paper, and head out the door. I've got to get to my mom.

When I walk out front, Jess is helping another man. He looks at her like she's a snack, and he's a starved man.

What the fuck is with all these men lately?

Chapter Twenty-Three

JESS

"WORK WAS WEIRD," I explain to the girls.

Lindsey, Brooke, Taylor, and I are addressing and stuffing Brooke's Save the Dates. Is this Taylor's first time hanging with us? Yes. Am I making her do manual labor? Yes.

But I gave her pizza and beer, and she seems happy so . . .

"How so?" Lindsey asks.

"I think I messed everything up, or at least everything in my head." I sigh. "I thought Julian was going to kiss me yesterday, and then he didn't. Then he told me he wanted to be just friends, but looked at me like he wanted to throw me into a sea of pillows and have his way with me." I sigh, remembering his heated gaze, and the way the goosebumps pebbled across my skin. "Then after my head was thoroughly confused, he left without saying anything. Becky came out a few minutes later and said 'he'll come around to loving you.'"

"What the fuck!" Taylor shouts.

We all start laughing.

"I don't know babe, maybe you should try just being his friend, ya know? If you really like him play the long game?" Brooke says.

"She has a point. You haven't ever really been in a real relationship. You don't normally care about the guys you hook up with, let alone have feelings. Maybe just step back and be his friend? Seems like he has been through a lot," Lindsey adds.

"I have nothing to add," Taylor mumbles, looking around, and we all laugh again.

"Yeah, maybe, anyway, thanks for coming and helping with this, Taylor! I know you barely know us, and I basically recruited you to do a stranger's wedding prep, but it's been fun getting to know you!" I smile at her.

"Girl, this is a million times better than being home right now. My roommate is the worst." She laughs.

"Oh no, can you move out?" I ask.

She sighs. "It's complicated. I live with Stephen? Remember the grouchy pants from the farm? Yeah, we are co-workers too."

"Oh. Wow. I can't wait to hear how that happened!" I chuckle.

"It's a long story, and I don't want to bore you guys the first time we hang out. I'll save it for the second time. Just know that this is way more fun than being home, and I'm happy to be here." She laughs.

"Okay, on a serious note, Mistletoe Meadows seems so fun," I say.

"Oh it is! But you know what else seems fun, owning a bookstore. Lindsey, how'd you land this place right above your bookstore? I love it in here!" Taylor asks.

"It was my grandma's. Came as a matching set, and there isn't a cute story behind it unfortunately," she says softly.

"Lindsey is being modest; she has put so much work into this place!" I interject.

"Well, either way, it's amazing Lindsey! You should be so proud of yourself! I'm sure it's not easy running a business and keeping this place clean, along with keeping this cutie happy and healthy!" Taylor says, gesturing to Scout and giving him an ear scratch.

"No, it isn't, but luckily I don't have a man to entertain, or a relationship to nurture, so that helps!" She laughs, but it isn't a fun laugh. It's a sad, pitiful laugh.

"You'll find someone someday!" I give her hand a gentle squeeze.

"I'm the perfect example honestly Linds, just stop looking for a guy and one will just fall in your lap!" Brooke laughs.

"Not everyone can meet the love of their life in a freak hiking accident, Brooke!" I scold jokingly.

"Eh, I know, I just mean the right person will come along when the time is right." She smiles at all of us.

I immediately feel annoyed, the same way I do with my sister Sarah. I love Brooke and Sarah, but when you're single, the cliches like, "when you know you know" are frustrating and don't make any fucking sense.

I know Brooke is on cloud nine right now though, so I keep my mouth shut . . . for once. This moment makes me realize I am growing up. I'm not the same girl I was before I moved to Rose Point, and I'm okay with that.

"The right time isn't right now? When I finally have my dream career? Living in the best city? With the coolest girl gang?" I gesture around to all of them.

Lindsey grabs my hand. "Sometimes your girl gang is the real prize, the real valuable relationship. As long as I have you guys, I'll never feel lonely or sad about a boy."

My eyes water slightly, but I blink and fight off the tears. "Bitch, don't ruin my makeup!"

We all laugh, and spend the rest of the night eating pizza and watching one of our favorite movies: *How to Lose a Guy in 10 Days.*

It's the perfect night, but my mind keeps drifting off to a six foot tall muscular hottie with a magical tongue. As much as I fight it, I can't stop thinking about him.

Chapter Twenty-Four

JULIAN

TELLING JESS I WANT to be just friends was a mistake.

I've spent the past two weeks working every shift with her, and it's confusing. We work so well together, you'd think we've always been partners in business.

I realize she's not technically my partner, but I value her opinions and the way we work together is seamless. Business is doing amazing. Jess started doing the classes to teach others how to make floral arrangements. We already had a bachelorette party, and Lindsey's romance book club took a class.

The "Build Your Own Bouquet" bar is doing well, and of course, lots of men are coming in to build arrangements with Jess. Every time they do I have to put my jealousy in check and remember she is doing her job.

Jess and I have been working together on the upcoming weddings, including Brooke's, and I even did interviews to hire another staff member, as today is Becky's last day.

I can't believe Becky is leaving, but I will say, it's good timing. If I have to listen to her talk to me about giving in and being with Jess one more time . . . I don't know what I'll do.

I'm going to miss Becky though. She was originally Hannah's friend, but she's been there for me ever since Hannah passed. I consider her my friend now. I wouldn't have been able to keep this business moving along and successful without her all these years.

She's trained Jess super well though. Everything she taught me, she taught Jess. But she taught Jess even more, because obviously I don't work directly with the flowers.

I think this is as ready as we can be for her departure.

We close up the shop, and everyone comes by to say goodbye to Becky. I grab a bottle of champagne from the back along with plastic cups to celebrate her new start.

Becky is shocked.

"Julian, breaking his own rules and drinking on the job!" she gasps.

"I'm not drinking on the job Becky, I'm drinking after the job. We are celebrating you. We are all so happy for you and your new start!" I hold up my plastic cup to cheers with her.

She starts crying.

Jess interrupts her crying, "May I say something?" She looks to me.

"Of course!" I reply.

"I just want to say how grateful I am to you Becky. You hired me and took a chance on a girl fresh out of a floral design class who had big dreams. I owe you my life, this life. The one where I live in my favorite city, hangout with my favorite people, and get to come to my dream job. I . . . I just hope you find the happiness you gave me in your next adventure." She lifts her cup up to cheers, and we all cheers to that.

"Much better with words than I am." I wink at Jess.

"Someone make sure these two get together at some point," Becky whines.

Jess turns bright red, and it immediately sends a wave of heat through my body.

"Becky, she is my employee, and I'm a professional. We've talked about this." I grind my teeth together, because her comment is embarrassing.

"Oh stop, none of these people would find you any less professional. There is clearly something here," she gestures between us, "and you're both single consenting adults."

"Anyways! To Becky's new beginning!" I hold up my cup again to cheers a third time, like an idiot, because I need to change the subject.

Once we get everything cleaned up, I text my mom to check on Jules.

> She's fine. Stop worrying, I'm paint-
> ing her nails before she heads to bed.
> Enjoy Becky's last night Julian.

> Are you sure? How are you feeling?
> You okay?

> Julian, I've finished my meds, I'm
> fine. Knock it off, son.

I roll my eyes, because I can totally hear that text in her voice.

Jess, Becky, and I head out to Stem Street Station for a drink to celebrate Becky's last night in town.

When we walk in, I have to swallow a huge lump in my throat, because this is where I first saw Jess.

That image of her demanding I take a shot with her comes flooding into my brain.

I push it deep down, because we are friends. Just friends. I have a kid. I'm her boss. I remind myself the same things over and over.

Becky, Jess, and I grab a booth and have a drink. We listen to Becky chat about all the things she is excited about.

I can't stop my eyes from wandering to Jess every few words though, since she's sitting directly across from me.

Her hair cascades down in waves framing her face, and those stunning blue eyes twinkle with mischief. The tights and heels she has on tonight, combined with that tight skirt, continue to make my cock twitch.

Life would be so much easier if I didn't know what was under there.

It's been almost a month since, and yet I can still remember every detail. I wonder if Jess can too? She was intoxicated, but so was I, and it still haunts me.

I wonder how I'll continue to work with her, and see her everyday, with this torturing me. I hope I eventually forget.

Becky gets a text, and starts typing, when Jess finally looks at me. She smiles, like this isn't absolutely torturing her like it is me.

"I think it's time for me to head out," Becky says when she finally looks up from her phone.

"Becky, I . . . " My voice trails off, as the emotion clogs my throat.

"Stop, Julian, you'll see me again soon, this isn't goodbye." She smiles sadly at me, while reaching over and giving my hand a squeeze.

"Right, okay, see you soon then," I whisper.

"See you soon." She smiles.

Becky leaves and I'm left there staring at Jess.

Jess sips her drink and smiles at me.

"Well, we should probably head out soon too, we've got a wedding tomorrow, remember?" I ask.

"How could I forget?" She laughs. "I've spent weeks planning and making those arrangements. Freaking Bridezilla, I hope she's happy."

I laugh lightly, knowing Jess absolutely knocked it out of the park with the arrangements. "I'm sure she will be. You did exactly what she wanted." I smile over at her, hoping she believes me when I say that she's killing it at work.

Jess slams back the rest of her drink and grabs her purse. "Alright, I'm ready when you are."

The way she says it, seductively, makes it sounds like we will be together after we leave here. We won't though. I can't.

I can't help but wonder if she's even interested anymore. It feels like she's flirty and seductive with everyone. Like, that's just her personality.

"What are you thinking about?" Jess asks.

"The wedding tomorrow . . ." I lie.

She gives me a look, like she knows I'm lying. But what am I supposed to say? Am I supposed to say *I think I'm falling for you, I can't stop thinking about you, your lips, the way you support me without trying* ... I'd sound insane.

She smirks, like she can read my fucking mind, and it drives me insane. Part of me is convinced she can, the way she always says the right thing. She always says what I need to hear.

"Do you regret it?" she asks.

"Regret what?" I question.

"That first night?" she whispers.

"Not at all, and I never could. I told you that I didn't regret it. How could I when it was so fucking amazing? I just . . . can't be what you need," I whisper.

I get up out of the booth, and reach for her hand to help her up.

She grabs my hand, and I immediately feel sparks. I don't want to let go of her hand, not now, and not ever.

I keep her hand in mine as I guide her out of the crowded bar.

When we get outside, I let go, as much as it pains me to.

"Let me walk you home? It's nearby if I remember right?" I ask, downplaying how I know exactly which building is hers.

"Yeah, I'm literally around the corner and up the stairs," she answers.

"Okay." We start walking. I'm following her lead.

We turn the corner, and Jess asks, "How's Jules?"

"She's great, thriving really. No thanks to me; the school and my mom see her more than I do," I admit sadly.

"You're doing your best Julian, and someday the store won't need you as much. You'll have enough competent employees that you can just only come in while Jules is in school. You're playing the long game, and Jules loves you and all you do for her," Jess explains.

And this is what I mean: she always knows what to say.

"Here we are, unless you're going to walk me upstairs." She laughs.

"Up the stairs we go," I say, as we start walking inside the building and up. "I didn't realize how close you were to the bar. Why'd we go all the way to my house that first night?" I chuckle.

"Because my 'house' is a studio apartment that was covered in boxes that first night, with a mattress on the floor and a nosy neighbor," she explains.

"Jess, are you saying you used me for a comfy bed?" I act shocked.

"No, I'm saying I used you for amazing orgasms, plural, or did you forget about that?" she purrs.

We reach her door.

"Jess, you're killing me. Quit bringing it up," I groan.

"You brought it up first by asking why we went to your house that night. I'm just reminding you of just how it was. Why's it killing you? You want to do it again?" She crawls her fingers up my chest, and wraps her hands around my neck.

"Jess ..." I whine.

"Yes, Julian?" she asks as she brings her face closer to mine.

I push her back toward the door to her apartment, forcing her against it.

"Jess . . . I can't do this," I groan.

"Say it again, and this time try to mean it," she whispers against my lips.

But I can't, so I do the stupidest thing, and I kiss her.

I kiss her hard. I kiss her with weeks of built up frustration and passion. I nip at her bottom lip, and suck it, before continuing to explore her mouth like it's the first time.

It kind of does feel like the first time though, because this time, I've got feelings, big feelings that I've tried to shove deep down.

Jess moans, "Julian."

After another second, she pulls away, pushing me back as she steps back. "I'm so sorry," she whispers. She heads into her apartment, and closes the door without another word.

I stare at the door a minute before turning to leave.

I am completely panicked. I thought she wanted me too. I thought after the conversation with my mom I was ready for this, that we were ready for this. I'm confused, and slightly frustrated, as I head back down the stairs, and home as fast as I can.

Chapter Twenty-Five

JESS

I stand there, back against my door, watching Julian basically take off running, and I can't help but feel totally miserable. I'm not what he needs. I'm not responsible or stable. He has a gorgeous daughter who deserves more than me. Hell, he deserves more than me.

I sit down on my bed, and place my head between my hands.

I felt like we were so good. We work so well together. He has been flirting with me. I thought we were good.

I think back on my conversation with Jules the other day, when we talked about losing our moms at a young age. The impact that has had on my life. I can't imagine what

Julian has gone through. I've felt this sense of connection to him from day one, like our shared sense of loss has brought us closer.

So why do I continue to push him away?

There is a knock on my door. I jump up excitedly, realizing he came back, and I can make things right. I swing the door open.

Only to be met with the face of Phyllis. Her dark brown hair is pinned up in curlers. She's got on pink floral pajamas with a purple robe on top, and she's wearing matching purple slippers.

Her face doesn't look angry though, to my surprise, and I try to hide my disappointment that she isn't Julian.

"May I come in?" she asks.

"Uh, I guess," I reply, moving to the side and gesturing inside.

She walks in and looks around. "I forgot how small this one is. You did good though, looks clean and nice."

"Uh, I didn't know I needed your approval?" I snap.

"Listen, I'm not here to argue, not tonight," she says somberly.

"Then why are you here at all?" I ask.

"That man, he's hot, and he likes you. But he is grieving, and grief . . . it's a hard thing to process. I just wanted to tell you, it's not your fault," she whispers.

"Phyllis, were you watching me?" I argue.

"Yeah, I always do, through my peephole," she admits.

"Phyllis, get a life!" I yell.

"I wish I could, kid." She laughs.

"Listen, I've been hard on you, but you're a good kid. You work hard, you take care of the people you love, both near and far. I wouldn't leave my cats with you if I left on vacation, but that could change, you have a lot of potential," she rants.

"Phyllis, could you get to the point? I'm tired," I whine.

"Jess, I don't know you well, but I know enough to know this: you and that man, you have something special. You have what most people crave," Phyllis explains.

"Good sexual chemistry?" I question.

"No, you idiot. You have love, the type of love that people search for. The kind that keeps you up at night. Where you balance each other so perfectly. Where he makes you want to settle down and be responsible, and you make him want to live and enjoy the little things again," she says.

"Phyllis, you couldn't have possibly got all of that from that one kiss," I scold.

"No, I got it from listening to your sorry ass on the phone every day since you moved in. Be the person you want to be Jess. Grow up, take responsibility, and wait for that man. The man of your dreams. Don't move on because you think he's rejected you once. Or because you think you're not enough," she continues.

"Phyllis, truly, this is sweet and all, but why do you care?" I ask.

"Because I've been in his shoes. I've been in them twice. I had the love of my life, and he died in a car accident. And somehow years later, I found love again, because a man was patient, and realized I was the one for him and fought for it. He patiently waited for me to be ready, and Jess, I carried a lot of guilt, because how could I move on? It took everything in me, but it was worth it. I got to have two great loves, and it was worth it." Tears run down her face now, and I immediately feel sad.

This woman, who has been yelling through my wall for a month, she's lonely.

"What happened to the second man?" I ask gently.

"We spent twenty-seven amazing years together, before he passed away from cancer. But those twenty-seven years we lived like every day might be our last. The biggest thing though, was he never tried to be better or more than my first love. He went to the cemetery with me. He supported me when I felt the guilt and grief coming in. You can do that too, if you want, if you think Julian is worth it." She wipes the tears from her face.

"Phyllis, do you know Julian?" I ask.

"My Bob was Hannah's uncle. We took Hannah in when she was teenager. Her parents had a lot of issues, and I'm not sure how Hannah turned out as well as she did given the circumstances. We were distraught when Hannah died, and Bob tried to get Julian to lean on us for support. He tried to get Julian to come talk to me, so I could tell him how grief never goes away, but it does get easier. He wouldn't though. He wanted to focus on Jules. He wasn't in a place to listen. When Bob died, Julian brought flowers to the funeral. Did a bunch of arrangements. He said it's what Hannah would've wanted. He's a sweet boy. I want him to find a happy ending. He can't live miserably forever . . ."

I can't process it all.

I lost my mom, but I don't even remember. I watched my dad grieve, but he never moved on, at least not that I know of. I can't fathom what Phyllis and Julian have been through. I really can't.

"Phyllis, I really, truly appreciate your insight. I do like Julian, a lot. We work well together, and he's the first guy I've felt . . . well, everything for. I want it to work out, and if it does, great. But I deserve happiness too. I don't always want to feel rejected, or like I'm not as good as what came before me . . ." My eyes water now, as I realize the weight of what I've been feeling. "I want him to be happy, but I want to be happy too," I cry.

"Can I hug you?" she asks.

I nod my head in response.

Phyllis walks over and gives me a hug.

"Have you ever lost someone, kid?" she asks.

"My mom died when I was little, but I don't remember. I bet she would know what to say or do now." I attempt to laugh, but it comes out watery and thin as tears stream down my face.

"Well, I never had kids. It wasn't in the cards for Bob and me. But I'll pretend to be your mom. You deserve every good thing in this life, but so does he. I think you guys could have it all . . . together, but you can't give up on it. Love like that is worth fighting for." She squeezes me.

I can't stop crying. I don't even know why. I just know I needed this hug more than I ever realized.

Chapter Twenty-Six

JULIAN

I WALK INTO MY house, confused. I thought I had a breakthrough with my mom in the hospital. I thought I was ready for Jess, or to at least try.

To see what was there. We work so well together. I thought I was ready for more. I clearly misread the signals though. I apparently lost all my ability to read a woman.

She pushed me away, and I couldn't get out of there faster.

I stand in my doorway, still holding my keys in my hand, as my mom comes around the corner, asking how my night was.

I just stand there a minute, trying to compose myself.

My mom looks worried. "You look like you just got dumped by a Hallmark movie."

"Didn't get dumped. You can't get dumped if you never got picked," I say sadly.

"Oof. That sounds like something you'd put on a mug," she mumbles.

"Don't tempt me." I laugh.

"Okay, well, spill. What happened?" she asks.

"I kissed Jess," I whisper.

"Jess? Like *the* Jess? The one we all love?" she questions.

"That's the one. I walked her home, head pounding, palms sweating, going over everything in my head the whole time. And then she pushed me away," I explain.

"Like push push? Or just stopped kissing you back?" She harasses me.

"I don't know a gentle nudge, maybe?" I say, confused by the memory.

"Oof. Classic 'I'm secretly in love with you but can't admit it because I'm panicking' kiss push." She laughs.

There is a brief moment of silence, where I can tell my mom wants to make another joke, but decides against it.

"You put yourself out there again, Julian. That's huge! Be proud of yourself," she says gently.

"Tell that to my ego. It's currently hiding under the table with my dignity and half of Jules' blueberry muffin." I laugh pathetically.

"Oh, no. I cleaned that muffin up hours ago." She chuckles. "Plus, you've survived worse. Remember when your kid told her entire class you cried during *Frozen 2*?"

"That was a deeply emotional movie about sisterhood and redemption," I say defensively.

"Sure it was," my mom says sarcastically. "You know, I've seen the way Jess looks at you . . ." my mom starts.

"Yeah, probably with pity. Like I'm a charity case in flannel." I sigh.

"No. Like she's trying really hard *not* to look at you too much," my mom explains. "I think some people build walls so high, they forget they're standing behind them. And Jess, she has walls, but so did you. Give her a minute to catch up. She doesn't have an awesome mom to nudge her along."

"So, what do I do now?" I ask, feeling slightly embarrassed that I'm a grown man asking my mom what to do next.

She smiles wide. "The same thing you tell Jules to do when she falls off her bike."

"Get back up and try again?" I let out a low chuckle, thinking of how my six-year-old could probably school me in getting back up again at this point.

"Get back up and try again." She smirks back at me, the telltale expression of a wise woman who knows she's right.

The next day Jess and I work the whole wedding together. In almost silence, both of us seem scared to mention anything on the off chance last night comes up.

We work well though, just like we always do.

We pull off the biggest wedding Blossom Bliss has ever seen. Bridezilla is squealing and happy as we drive away.

After a long, quiet drive back to the store, I put the shop van in park, as Jess says, "I'm sorry, I panicked."

"Believe it or not, I panicked too," I answer with a gentle smile.

I get out of the car, and as we start unloading, I end up lost in my own thoughts.

I've held back from telling Jess I love her. It still feels like I don't deserve to love her the way I do. I couldn't give that kind of love to Hannah, and it's eaten at me all these years.

But I have this chance now, to love Jess that way. To do things right this time.

An idea forms, but I need some time and help to execute it. Something I hate asking for, but at this point, I'd do anything for Jess.

"Can you meet me at Petal Patch Acres tomorrow at sunrise?"

Chapter Twenty–Seven

JESS

I SPENT THE ENTIRE night anxious, unsure of what Julian was thinking, telling me to come meet him here.

It's a foggy morning when I arrive at Petal Patch Acres. I'm not a morning person, by any means, so being here at sunrise is asking a lot of me.

There is a small sign by the front gate that reads: Jess, meet me in the greenhouse, by the peonies.

I make my way down the path to the greenhouse.

Fog curls around the glass panes. The world is quiet, washed in a soft glow.

I open the door and step inside. The greenhouse is supposed to be empty, or at least it was the last time we were here. But something's different this morning, and my body hums with excitement.

I open the door, stop, and blink.

Everywhere, every table, every hook, every inch of the space is filled with flowers. Not just random bouquets, but *our story*, told in blooms.

Peonies, from the first wedding we worked together.

Wild daisies, just like the ones I wove into his daughter's flower crown that summer afternoon.

Lavender, his favorite scent, the one I always tease him about.

And at the very center, a massive arch of white roses and forget-me-nots, twisting upward like a living sculpture.

I walk closer, brushing my fingertips along the petals, trying not to cry.

A small card hangs from the arch. I reach up and pull it down.

"You once told me flowers were meant to say what words can't. So I'll say it this way: Be with me. Not because you're scared, but because you're home."

Behind me, the door cracks open, and Julian walks in. He stands there, holding a single stem. A ranunculus, the bloom I once said was "too beautiful to last."

"You were right. They don't last. Not unless you keep showing up to work and taking care of them." He cracks a smile.

"You did all this?" I ask.

"Took me all night. I had to steal a few stems from the back cooler. Don't tell the boss." He winks.

I laugh through tears. "This is insane, Julian."

"Yeah, so is falling for someone when I swore I couldn't," he whispers, placing the ranunculus on the table beside me. "But here we are." He gestures around the greenhouse.

I look around again, taking in the gesture. The scent, the color, and the meaning behind it.

"You made a whole garden out of us," I whisper.

"I just wanted you to see what happens when someone finally commits, when someone stays," he says softly, taking my hand in his.

I kiss him, softly at first, and then like I've finally found my place.

Light spills in from the roof as I grab his biceps and pull him further into me.

He kisses down my neck and the hollow of my shoulder.

Instant heat finds its place between my thighs. My breath becomes erratic, and when I look at him again, his eyes are glazed with need.

I can't even bear to look at him, because every time I see his lips, panting with desire, the urge to rip off his pants nearly overwhelms me. I'm trying to take things slow and make this time different. Different from every time I've had before this.

So instead, I kiss him again. I kiss him everywhere, and ignore the fierce pounding of my blood every time he moans.

The table next to us has a small opening, and Julian lifts me up and puts me up on top of the table with ease, as we continue kissing.

"How do you know Stephen, or Taylor, or another Petal Patch employee won't come in here?" I ask nervously.

"I threw Stephen a hundred bucks to make sure no one started their day until I gave him the green light," he replies with a wink. "Not that I expected *this*, but I did want us to have some privacy."

He lifts me up and shimmies off my skirt, falling to his knees in the process.

I run my fingers through his hair and give it a quick pull.

He smirks at me, before pushing my panties to the side, and swiping his tongue over me, top to bottom.

"Jesus, you're so wet right now." He glides his fingers up and down, and then pushes one inside me to emphasize his point. I let my knees drop open even more, encouraging him. His fingers circle my opening, and I groan out loud before he slides two fingers inside me. I rock into him, and gasp.

Bucking beneath him, as he dives in, flicking my clit with his tongue. "God, you're perfect," I moan as he continues to drive his tongue at the exact spot I need him most.

He removes his tongue, as I whimper in protest, but quickly replaces his tongue with his thumb on my clit as he applies more pressure, and my head starts to spin.

He stands up and kisses me as he continues applying pressure to my clit. My breath comes out in small gasps, in rhythm with the thrust of my hips as I grind into him more.

I hear him moan, and then hear the soft thud of his own pants hitting the floor, as he starts stroking his own length with his free hand.

My eyes open wide to watch him, his gaze dark as he grips his cock tight, and that's all it takes for me.

All the pressure builds in my abdomen, and when he feels my muscles tightening, he lets go of his grip on his cock. He falls back to his knees, grips my thighs tight, and drives his tongue in again like a starved man.

He buries his face between my legs and licks hard as I arch against him, my hands gripping the edge of the table. I bring my knees over his shoulders, to get him as deep as I can. When finally, fireworks explode behind my eyes, as I let go. I cry out, letting the entire world fall away.

He doesn't let up though, not for a moment until I reach down, grip his hair, and pull him back up.

"Come here," I gasp, and he knows exactly what I mean. He rises quickly, pulling me forward and driving into me. Like he might die if he doesn't get there soon enough.

He thrusts into me, and I'm suddenly so full. I forgot just how big Julian is.

I cry out at the pleasure.

He reaches up, grabbing my face with one hand, and kisses me tenderly.

"You okay?" he whispers.

"God, yes," I mumble, and he laughs before slowly moving back into me.

Push in, slow drag out, repeat. I want to do this for the rest of my life, and with only him.

"Jess, you feel so fucking good," he moans, before quickening his pace. He starts moving faster, like he's losing control. I love seeing him like this.

His fingers move to my clit, light but fast as he continues to drive in.

I slide forward, the table starting to get uncomfortable.

Because he is in tune with my every need and desire, he picks me up off the table. Lifting me up under my ass, and pulling out, and setting me on the ground, before flipping me around.

I lean over as he slides himself back in, and I cry out again.

He thrusts into me from behind, as I lean over, just a little bit, using a nearby pole to prop myself up.

He moves his hand up to my neck, squeezing gently before moving my head to the side. He kisses me passionately while continuing to slowly thrust into me.

"God, Jess, look how well you take me," he moans, moving my head in the direction of the glass window next to us.

I can see the reflection of us, and it's the hottest thing I've ever seen.

He keeps one hand on my neck and starts moving faster again.

"Oh, fuck, Julian. I'm close again, don't stop," I moan.

He picks up the pace even more, heat rushing up my body, my muscles stiffen, everything is wound so tight I feel like I might snap in half.

"I'm gonna–" I gasp, and then I clench around him, and as my head digs backward into him. My back arches as he reaches around, grabbing my breasts hard.

My orgasm intensifies as I spasm around him. My core grips him tight.

"Fuck," Julian hisses. His thrusts are hard, uneven, but perfect as he finds his own release.

We both come down, breathing hard.

He slowly pulls out and turns me around to push me up against the cool, fogged glass and kisses me. When his eyes open, he looks as stunned as I feel.

I'm not sure why. It's not like we haven't done this before. This time just felt like *more*.

Chapter Twenty-Eight

JULIAN

I'VE HAD SEX WITH Jess before, in a comfortable bed, and it was amazing. But it was raunchy, and we barely knew each other.

So having sex with Jess while I have a million feelings in my chest is next-level. It was romantic and hot, and everything Jess is.

However, I told Jess that I wanted to be with her, and she never really gave me a straight answer. The sex was perfect, but does that mean we're doing this? I wish I could get a read on her.

I know everything isn't going to be sunshine and rainbows from here on out. But I'm ready to give things my all with Jess.

The next day I wake up full of anxiety. I had yesterday off with Jules. Today though, she's off to school, and I'm off to work . . . with Jess.

I've got a knot of anxiety in my stomach, because how will I work with Jess now? Will it be awkward? What if I ruined our amazing work dynamic with all my feelings?

Luckily, I don't have to worry too much, because upon arrival, it's busy. Busiest day we've had all year. You'd think it was Valentine's Day by the looks of this place.

Halfway through the shift, Jess and I share a bewildered look, as she asks, "What the heck is going on today?"

We laugh, and keep pushing through.

I end up calling my mom and asking her to pick up Jules and handle dinner, as I explain what's going on.

My mom is, of course, so excited, because I originally told her I was only working while Jules was in school this week, and I didn't need her help.

Jess ends up staying late too. With four of us all working together, we manage to get everything cleaned up and closed on time still.

The other employees head out while I run to the back to grab my stuff. I come back out and look around, the "Open" sign hangs crooked, one light still buzzing. I make a mental note to fix it tomorrow. There are buckets of half-wilted roses and daisies glowing in the soft lamplight.

And Jess stands in the middle of the store, looking like she is either going to bolt or burst into tears.

"What's wrong?" I ask, making my way over to her.

She holds up a hand, gesturing to me to stop. I do, and I stand there, unsure where to put my hands, or what to do.

"I think . . . I think I love you," she whispers.

She'd said it like someone throwing a match onto a pile of dry leaves . . . terrified and impulsive. But I can tell it's entirely sincere.

And now she is just standing in the middle of my flower shop like she is wishing the floor would open up and swallow her whole.

I don't move. I can't. I just stare at her, trying to make sense of those three little words that are still hanging in the air.

"Do you really mean that?" I finally manage. My voice doesn't sound like mine. I'm too soft, too careful.

"I . . . yeah. I think I do. Which is . . . terrifying. So please don't make me say it again or I might throw up on the lilies." She giggles, wiping the tears from her cheek.

That makes me laugh. God, she always does that, cracks a joke right when I'm about to fall apart.

I want to tell her not to be scared. But the truth is, I am. Terrified, actually. Because I know what love can do, how it can leave you hollowed out, trying to raise a kid and keep a flower shop running on caffeine and denial.

"You always go for humor when you're scared," I say instead.

"Yeah, well, you always hide behind flowers," she shoots back, pointing to my hand.

That hit harder than she probably meant it to. But I look down and sure enough, I am holding a tulip. A white one. My hands do that on their own these days, find something to tend, to protect, when my heart starts racing.

I look up at her. "I don't know how to do this," I finally say softly.

"Good," she says. "Because if you did, I'd probably run screaming."

My phone buzzes. It's a text from my mom.

> You coming home soon?

I glance at Jess. She sees the message.

"Let's go. You need to get home. Jules is waiting." She smiles.

I hesitate, staring at the tulip in my hand. Then I hold it out to her. "Here, keep it."

She raises an eyebrow. "Pretty sure the boss would have opinions about that."

"Good thing the boss is just me," I reply, as she grabs the tulips, giggling.

We walk out into the night. She stands there, holding the tulip like it's something breakable.

I can't help but think, maybe love doesn't bloom all at once. Maybe it just... keeps showing up. And for the first time in a long time, I don't feel like hiding behind flowers.

When I arrive home the house smells like burnt popcorn and impending judgement.

My mom and Jules are on the couch, feet tucked under a blanket, remote in mom's hand, a bowl of popcorn in Jules'.

"You're smiling!" Jules shouts.

"Am I not allowed to smile in my own house?" I laugh.

"Not like that. That's your *weird smile*. The one you get when something happens but you don't want to tell me." She crosses her arms in front of her, and makes a grumpy face.

I kick off my shoes, set my keys in the bowl by the door, and try to look casual. "Maybe I'm just in a good mood."

"Uh-huh," she said, drawing the word out. "Does this good mood have anything to do with Jess?"

I turn and glare at Mom, because there is no way my six-year-old came up with that idea herself.

"Why would you think that?" I demand.

My mom starts chuckling, but I notice her silence, and glare at her again.

"You only look like that when she's around. Also, you smell like flowers." Jules smiles, proud of herself. Like she said everything the way my mom told her to.

"Because I *own* the shop." I defend myself, but my mom is already smirking.

"But she likes you!" Jules squeals.

"Mom!" I shout.

"What? I didn't tell her!" My mom defends back, laughing.

"Dad. I've seen the way she looks at you, she looks at you like Aladdin looks at Jasmine. She has a crush!" Jules giggles.

I rub a hand over my face. "You're supposed to be a kid. Kids don't notice that kind of thing."

She pops a handful of popcorn into her mouth. "I'm not a kid. I'm six. That's, like, practically a romance expert. Bluey and Bingo are like, six, and they know all about romance!"

I snort. "God, help me."

My mom continues to just laugh.

For a second, the room gets quiet, the only sound being the movie playing on the TV. Then Jules softly says, "You like her too? Don't you?"

I go sit down on the arm of the couch, next to her, staring at the floor.

"Yeah, I do," I whisper.

"Then what's the problem?" she asks.

My mom finally takes a hint, grabs the popcorn bowl from Jules, and heads to the kitchen, leaving me and Jules alone.

What's the problem ... well there are a few hundred answers. I'm her boss. I've already lost one love forever; I don't know if I can handle it again. You deserve stability, not another heartbreak in progress.

But she is looking at me with that steady, hopeful gaze that used to belong to her mother. So I say, "I don't know."

She smiles a little. "You always tell me to be brave, even when stuff's scary."

Touché.

I sigh, and then reach over and wrap my arm around her. "You're too smart for your own good."

"Genetics." She smiles up at me.

I can't help but laugh hysterically at that.

We watch the rest of the movie together, her little head on my shoulder.

But the whole time, I kept thinking about Jess standing in the glow of the shop lights, holding that white tulip.

And the thought doesn't scare me anymore.

Chapter Twenty-Nine

JESS

I SPENT THE ENTIRE night dissecting every word I'd said.

Every. Single. Word.

Somewhere between the third replay of *"I think I love you"* and my fourth cup of tea, I started googling "can you die from emotional mortification" and "how to quit your job without facing your boss-slash-crush."

Spoiler alert: Google was unhelpful.

By the time I got to the shop the next morning, I'd come up with at least six escape plans. None of them were good. Option A: fake appendicitis. Option B: join witness protection. Option C: move to Iceland and raise goats.

Unfortunately, Option D: "act normal" was the only one that didn't require a passport or perjury.

The bell above the door chimes as I walk in. The shop is quiet today, sunlight coming through the window, catching on petals and vases. It smells like lavender and impending awkwardness.

I don't see Julian yet. I exhale, half relieved, half disappointed.

I set my bag down, and started trimming stems just to have something to do. My hands are shaking like I had espresso for breakfast instead of sheer panic.

I told him I loved him.

He didn't run.

He gave me a tulip.

Which, in the grand language of flowers, probably meant something like "hopeful beginnings" or "prepare to panic, emotional disaster incoming." I should know the meaning behind a tulip, and I'm kicking myself now for not googling that last night instead.

The back door opens, and Julian walks out.

"Morning," he says in that low, steady voice that somehow makes my stomach do Olympic-level gymnastics.

I freeze mid-snip. "Hey," I say, trying very hard to sound like a person who didn't confess her undying love twelve hours ago.

He looks … different. Softer, maybe. He is holding a cup of coffee in one hand, and an iced tea in the other. He offers me the tea.

"Peace offering," he says.

I blink at it. "For what?"

"For whatever awkwardness you've spent the last eight hours inventing." He smirks.

Okay, so maybe he knows me too well.

I take the cup, our fingers brushing just enough to make my brain short-circuit.

"Thanks," I murmur.

We stand there for a beat. The world smells like coffee, roses, and something brand new.

He finally breaks the silence. "So... are we okay?"

I bite my lip. "Define okay."

He smiles, slow and sure. "Still talking. Still working. Still ... whatever this is."

I nod, heart thudding. "Yeah. We're okay."

He nods in agreement nervously. "Okay, it's not that I don't . . . I know what you said yesterday, I just need some time?"

"I get it, Julian. Really, I do." I try to force a relaxed smile to put him at ease.

He steps behind the counter, and starts sorting stems like it was any other day. Like the world hadn't quietly tilted on its axis.

But when I catch him sneaking a look at me over the lilies, that warm, unguarded look, I realize maybe things don't have to go back to normal.

Maybe they could be *better*.

That afternoon as I'm packing up to leave, Julian catches me on my way out.

"Jess, do you want to have dinner tomorrow night?" he asks.

"Like, a date?" I ask nervously.

He laughs. "Well, not entirely. Jules will be there."

"Okay." I smile.

I stand in Julian's kitchen, trying not to look too out of place. The room smells faintly of burnt garlic bread and something tomato-based that had my stomach growling ten minutes ago. I'm holding a bottle of wine I grabbed from the corner store, hoping the label looked more *"casually charming"* than *"grabbed at the last second."*

Julian is at the stove, sleeves rolled up, brow furrowed in concentration. Jules stands on a stool beside him, proudly stirring a bowl of salad with both hands.

"You know," I say, arching an eyebrow, "most people wash the salad before ... finger painting it."

Jules looks at me, unbothered. "Daddy says germs build character."

"That's not exactly what I said," Julian begins to say, but Jules cuts him off.

"I'm full of character!" she declares, puffing her chest.

I laugh, and Julian turns and looks at me. Not in the obvious, hungry way men sometimes do, but with a quiet surprise, as if my laughter had knocked something loose in him.

"Thanks for coming," he says after a moment, turning back to the sauce. "Jules has been insisting we host a 'fancy dinner.'"

"This is fancy," Jules says happily. "You even lit a candle."

His eyes dart to the lone tealight flickering beside a ketchup bottle. "Mood lighting," he says, which a chuckle. "Very Michelin star dad of me."

"What's Michelin?" Jules asks.

"It's like a gold star for restaurants," Julian explains.

"Then I give Daddy *five* gold stars!" Jules shouts.

"Careful," I say, "Or he'll get cocky."

Julian smiles, that quiet half-smile I see at the shop sometimes. It is disarming in the worst way.

By the time we sit down to eat, the garlic bread is beyond burnt, the pasta is soft, and the salad crunches ominously. But I smile anyway, because it's edible, and it's the effort that counts. Plus my own dad's spaghetti is equally as awful, and I used to eat that weekly.

Jules twirls a forkful of spaghetti and says, "You know, florists are not great at cooking."

We all laugh.

"Well." His eyes glisten. "Hopefully Jess will still come to dinner again."

It was said lightly, teasingly, but the words caught somewhere deeper. He must have noticed the flicker of hesitation, because his voice softens.

"I mean, Jules would really like that," he says softly.

"I would!" Jules pipes up, sauce smeared across her cheeks. "Next time we can make pizza! I'll even wash some of the lettuce."

I smile at Jules, and pat her little hand. "Some is a good start."

I look back at Julian again, and this time I linger, a heartbeat too long, just enough for my chest to tighten in that strange, unwelcome way.

After dinner, Jules yawns her way through half a story before wandering off toward her room. The house feels instantly quieter, smaller somehow. I help clear the table while Julian rinses plates, sleeves rolled to his forearms.

"You're good at this," I say after a while.

He glances at me. "Cooking?"

"No." I hesitate. "This. The whole ... life thing."

He huffs a soft chuckle. "Some days. Other days I burn dinner and hope Jules doesn't tell her teacher the next day."

Still, he makes it look easy. The balance of it all, the warmth and chaos and ordinary love that fills every space of their home.

I lean against the counter, tracing the rim of my glass. "You make it look... safe."

Julian turns the tap off. The room hums with the sound of the city outside: traffic, distant laughter, the muffled patter of rain starting against the window.

"You don't have to run, you know," he says quietly. "Not every good thing needs an exit strategy."

My heart stutters for a moment.

"That's dangerous talk for a florist," I say finally, my voice low. "We're trained to make beauty that never lasts."

"Maybe this time, it could. Maybe it's just about showing up," he whispers.

He reaches for the same plate I do, and our hands brush. But neither of us pull away. The warmth of his skin lingers longer than it should, spreading up my arm like something alive.

I exhale slowly, aware of the little tealight candle burning low on the table, of the rain outside, of him.

And for the first time in a long while, I don't feel the urge to run.

I have a tea party with Jules and her stuffies, and then lay in her bed reading her a book. Julian lingers like he doesn't know what happens next, or how to do this bedtime routine with an extra set of hands.

I finish reading the story to Jules, my arm wrapped around her tight. I give her a squeeze.

"Can you stay forever?" Jules whispers while hugging me.

"Oh, I don't know, I think you'd get sick of me if I was around forever, bug," I reply.

"Maybe I'd call you big bug then!" She giggles.

I giggle at her little reference. "Maybe. Get some sleep. I'll see you again soon." I kiss her head.

"Like Frosty the Snowman?" she whispers.

"Like Frosty the Snowman," I promise.

I exit the room, so Julian can say goodnight to his little girl. I head down the hall and start putting my shoes on.

Julian comes out. "What are you doing?" he asks.

"Oh, I thought it was bedtime?" I explain.

"I mean, is it your bedtime too? Or do you want to watch a movie with me?" he asks.

I smile. "I'd love to watch a movie with you." I throw my stuff back down, running over and leaping on the couch.

"I love this couch," I whisper as I grab a blanket off the back.

"The truth finally comes out . . . you're using me for my couch." He laughs.

"No, never! I just miss having a couch." I chuckle, tossing a pillow at him, as he sits down next to me with the remote.

"You don't have a couch?" he asks.

"Nope, studio apartment. Just a bed," I sadly express.

He stares at me a minute, and for some reason, this feels like the most intimate thing I've ever done.

I've never just snuggled someone on a couch; they've always wanted more. Or expected more. Julian's arm is around me, as I move the blanket to share with him.

"What do you want to watch?" he whispers.

"I'll watch whatever!" I tell him.

"What's your favorite movie?" he asks.

"My favorite?" I question.

"Yeah, I want to know all your favorites," he says.

"Well, Sarah told me my mom's favorite movie was *Sleepless in Seattle*. So I've watched it probably a hundred times, and I would say it's my favorite based on that fact alone," I explain.

"*Sleepless in Seattle* it is," he says, pressing the buttons to find it and turn it on.

"Really? You don't mind watching a romantic comedy?"I ask.

"Why would I mind?" he questions.

"I don't know, I guess I just thought most guys don't like romantic comedies," I explain.

"I'm not like most guys," he says with a wink.

I laugh, and we snuggle together as the movie starts to play.

Chapter Thirty

JULIAN

I WON'T LIE. I had no idea what *Sleepless in Seattle* was or what it was about prior to starting this movie.

I get a little choked up at the end. I didn't know I would be emotional. But the single dad element has me feeling some type of way.

I'm trying not to cry in front of Jess the first time we watch a movie together.

Her head lays on my chest, and we haven't said but a few words the whole movie. It's nice though. I've forgotten how nice it is to just relax with someone you love at the end of a long day.

The word slams into my chest. Love.

I just thought about Jess being the person I love.

I'm in love with Jess.

It scares me to open up and let someone in, to not just my life, but Jules as well.

I've gotten to know Jess well though. If this doesn't work out for some reason, I know she will still care about Jules. After tonight, I'm honestly wondering if she actually likes Jules more than me …

"Jess," I whisper.

"Yeah?" she answers.

"Can we make this thing official?" I ask nervously.

She sits up and turns around toward me. "What do you mean?" she asks groggily.

"Like, I asked the other day at the greenhouse, but never really got an answer. So I'll just ask the old-fashioned, cheesy way. Will you be my girlfriend?" I question. As soon as the words leave my mouth, I immediately want to take them back. I'm a grown man, with a child. Having to label her as my girlfriend feels silly. It also feels like not enough, when I have a kid in the picture.

Jess just smiles. "Yeah."

"I just mean, like, we won't date other people. On the off chance you lose interest, I can't hurt Jules . . ." I start rambling.

"Julian, I said yes. I'm all in this, with you *and* Jules. Plus, I really don't see this ending or not working out," she explains.

"I like the sound of that," I say, and I reach over, grab her face with both my hands and kiss her.

It's tender and passionate, and my chest feels like it could explode from happiness. Which is crazy because three months ago, I thought I'd never be happy again.

I break away, and Jess looks at me with tears brimming her eyes.

"What's wrong?" I ask.

"You make a million decisions that mean nothing, and then one day you make a decision that changes everything," she says, quoting a line from *Sleepless in Seattle*.

I laugh. "I'm going to check on Jules. Do you want to stay the night? The only catch is . . . I don't want Jules to see you in the morning, so you'd have to leave pretty early."

"At least you warned me this time," she jokes.

"I'm glad we can laugh about it now," I say.

I run down the hall to check on Jules. She's of course sound asleep in her bed, cuddling with Professor Peanut. I give her a quick kiss on the forehead, and close the door behind me as I exit the room.

Jess is in the hall waiting for me. I smile at her, grab her hand, and lead her to my room. When we get there, I close the door behind her, and push her up against it.

"I know I didn't really respond the other day to you. It really threw me off guard. And when I asked if we were okay the next day, I know I should've mentioned it but I still just didn't know what to say. But, Jess, I think I love you too," I whisper against her lips.

Then I press my lips to hers, and it never gets old kissing Jess.

Her lips are soft and tender, and every time I kiss her it feels like time pauses. The air thickens with anticipation, and every beat of my heart becomes loud enough to hear.

Every time we kiss, I get a wave of nervous energy. It's a mix of excitement and fear, fear that I'm doing something wrong, fear of the unknown, but also the thrill of finally crossing that invisible line, and letting myself be happy.

As I move closer, everything else fades away. The sounds, even thoughts, vanish, while the rest of my senses heighten. I can feel warmth radiating off the closeness of her skin, the electric pull of Jess. The pull I always feel whenever she's around.

I've kissed Jess before, but this time feels different. It feels like a promise. The world seems to tilt, and a rush of warmth floods my chest, melting every ounce of anxiety into something gentle and bright. My stomach flips, and my hands don't quite know where to go, and yet somehow it still feels perfectly natural. Like I've discovered a language that doesn't need words.

When she finally pulls back, there's a small, shared silence. Our eyes meet. We share a shy smile. My heart races. And I realize that everything has subtly changed.

Chapter Thirty-One

JESS

I KNOW THE FIRST thing I think about after kissing Julian should not be Phyllis, but for some reason I can't help but think, *I'm so happy I listened to her.*

What if I never let myself experience this type of love?

I smile at Julian, after having a kiss that leaves my knees weak and arms shaking slightly.

Julian grabs under my ass, and lifts me up against the door, before turning me and carrying me to the bed.

He drops me onto the plush covers, and climbs on top of me, smiling the entire time. To think a few weeks ago, I thought this man had never smiled before, and now he can't stop.

Knowing I'm the reason for that joy, that smile, is something I will never take for granted. I want that smile plastered on his face for the rest of my life.

He deserves so much happiness.

He kisses me again, but this time it isn't tender or full of love. This time it's full of passion, full of need.

His hands roam my body, before finding their way to my skirt. He hikes my skirt up to my hips as he kisses down my neck.

I moan. I can't form a single word or thought. This man has me in a trance.

He moves down between my thighs, shoving my thong to the side and diving his tongue in, immediately finding my clit.

He moans, and it vibrates in all the right places.

"Oh, god, yes, Julian," I cry out. He comes up and locks eyes with me.

"You have to be quiet this time. Think you can handle that, babe?" He winks.

I bite my lip. I can be quiet. It'll be hard with this man, but I can do it. I nod my head.

"Good girl," he whispers, before kissing my thigh, and disappearing between my thighs again.

I grab his hair and rock my hips into him. It feels too good.

I bring my arm up and put my hand over my mouth, moaning softly into it.

Julian continues to caress my clit with his tongue. Finding the right spot, over and over.

All of the pressure starts to build deep in my core, but I'm not ready yet.

I grab his hair and pull him up to me. I give him one quick kiss, before flipping him onto his back.

I kiss my way down his neck before sliding off the bed and unbuttoning his pants. I slide them off him carefully, taking his pants and boxer briefs down with me. I throw them across the room, and grip his thighs while getting on my knees in front of him.

I wink at Julian before grabbing his cock and taking him deep, as he cries out.

I release him and look up at him through hooded eyes. "Be quiet, Julian." I wink, and then take him deep again.

I swirl around the tip and take him deep, over and over. Eventually I gag slightly at the size of him. I keep forgetting just how massive Julian is.

He pulls my hair, as I start to gently caress his balls.

"Get your fucking ass up here babe," he says, gently pulling me.

I stand up letting the rest of my skirt fall to the floor, and then sliding my thong off and letting it fall to the floor too.

"God, you're beautiful," he whispers.

My whole face feels hot. I climb up over him on my hands and knees, until I'm hovering over him. I kiss him, as I line myself up with his cock, before slowly and achingly dropping down.

"Oh, god, Jess," he mumbles.

I feel so powerful and in control, and I fucking love seeing him come undone under me.

I ride him, grinding into him, in slow, concentrated movements.

I take in and savor every inch of Julian. The pleasure is almost too much to bear, as I move up and down against him.

He reaches up, grabbing my hair with both hands, and pulls me down to kiss him hard, while I ride him.

He pulls away, and flips me over onto my back with ease, and then continues moving in and out, hitting my clit in the right way.

"Oh, Julian, I'm close," I whisper in his ear, and then nip at his earlobe. He moves his mouth down to my neck and moans into it. I wrap my legs around him to let him get even deeper.

"Oh that's it," I cry out.

He covers my mouth with his, just as I'm about to come undone. Kissing me hard as the pressure keeps building. I want to completely lose myself in him, so I let go. My legs are shaking around him as I see stars.

"God, yes, Julian," I whisper before biting his lip and sucking. He reaches down and grips my ass in his hands, lifting me up slightly, and drives into me at the perfect angle as I climax. He doesn't stop, and continues to thrust into me, finding his release too.

When we both come down from our high, Julian licks up my neck, nips at my earlobe, and whispers, "You're fucking perfect."

Chapter Thirty-Two

JULIAN

THE NEXT MORNING WE get Jess out the door before Jules wakes up. I kiss her and let her know that hopefully someday she can just stay here with us.

"You're a good dad Julian. I'll leave as many times as I need to keep it that way," she says, before kissing me one more time and heading off.

The next month and a half pass in the blink of an eye. The days don't move evenly, but they bend and blur. One minute I'm packing lunches, wiping down the counter, and answering my child's question about dinosaurs. The next minute my phone buzzes and I get a message, a small beam of light from Jess and the world seems to tilt. The hum of the refrigerator becomes background music to a pulse of excitement.

I find myself living in two tempos at once: the steady, practical rhythm of routines, and the shimmering quickness of something new unfolding. Time stretches when we are apart. How can an afternoon feel so long? Then time collapses and moves too quick when we finally get to be alone again. An hour together feels like only a handful of breaths.

There's sweetness to the contrast. I'm folding laundry with a secret smile, and cooking dinner while remembering the way her voice sounded that morning. My tasks don't disappear, but they soften at the edges, as if touched by her faint glow.

At night, after Jules is asleep, I text Jess until too late, the hours slipping by unnoticed. The clock says it's midnight, but it doesn't feel like a loss. Instead, it feels as if love has found a way to weave itself quietly through the fabric of my every day.

Sometimes Jess stays here, having dinner with Jules and me. She always leaves in the early morning hours before

Jules wakes up. It all feels like a dream that I haven't woken up from yet.

We hired two more people at work, one full-time, and one part-time. I had Jess help with every part of the hiring process. We still haven't told any of the employees we are dating yet, but I'm trying to shift and let Jess handle a bit more. It's her passion, and she's the lead florist.

I've only been working hours while Jules is at school, and it's been so nice to spend more time with Jules.

My mom still comes around and babysits occasionally, or comes for dinner at our house.

It's honestly felt like the last two weeks especially are too good to be true. I keep waiting for the other shoe to drop, for something bad to happen.

Jess calls me the week of Brooke's wedding. "My family is in town for the wedding, and I want you to meet them. If you can?" she asks nervously.

"Of course, I'd do anything for you," I reply.

Jess has gone home twice to see her sister and dad, but I haven't gone with her, not because I don't want to, but the timing just didn't work out.

I know she is nervous about me meeting them. She cares immensely about what her dad and her sister think. I know through the phone, they haven't been particularly happy that Jess ended up with a single dad, who also happens to be her boss. But I'm hopeful that once they know me, and my story, and see the way Jess and I are together they will understand.

At least that's what I have to tell myself now.

It's a Thursday evening. Jess and I have been working so hard on Brooke's wedding florals since neither of us can be the one to deliver them. With Jess and I both in the wedding it's caused a lot more planning and scheduling then normal.

However, we decide to take the night completely off to enjoy the time with her family.

Everyone is coming to my house, so I spend the entire afternoon cleaning with Jules. We make tacos for everyone because I have a great crockpot recipe and don't have to worry about messing it up too much.

As I put tortilla chips and salsa in bowls, Jules comes up to the corner and asks, "Why is this dinner so special Dad?"

I wipe my hands on the towel next to me, and kneel down to her level.

"You know how you are very special to me?" I ask her.

"Yeah!" Jules squeals.

"And you know how Jess is very special to us? How we want her to be part of our family someday?" I ask her.

"Like we want her to be my new mom?" she questions.

My heart sinks. I guess we haven't fully talked about what it would look like if Jess was part of our family.

"No one will ever replace your mom, but she would be a mother-figure. She'd do all the things a mom does, if she wanted to," I try to explain.

"Okay, but what about dinner?" she asks, confused.

"Well, dinner is important because Jess loves her family, her dad and sister, and we want them to also be part of our family someday." I struggle to explain the concept of a blended family to my daughter.

"Like Grandma kinda?" she asks.

"Yeah, kind of like Grandma." I smile.

"Okay, I hope I like them." She giggles.

"I'm sure you will, they helped make Jess who she is," I say.

"And I love love love Jess!" Jules yells.

"Yeah, me too." I smile.

"You love Jess too?" Jules asks.

"Yeah sweetie, I do." I kiss her cheek, and give her a hug.

"Like you loved Mommy?" Jules whispers sadly.

"It's a different kind of love sweetie, but I do hope we can be a family someday," I whisper, my eyes filling with tears.

I need to keep it together.

The doorbell rings, and Jules and I answer the door. It's just Jess for now, who looks nervous, scared, or maybe both.

It's hard to tell.

I give Jess a kiss, and then run to continue setting the table. I'm worried it's set too perfectly, and continue fidgeting with it.

"Babe, it's fine," Jess says, walking over and rubbing my shoulder gently.

"I want this to be perfect for you," I whisper.

"You're perfect for me, and that's all that matters," Jess says, kissing me again.

Jules is looking out the front window. "They're here! They're here! Can I open the door?" she squeals.

"Not yet, Jujubee! Remember to be polite, and say nice to meet you," I remind her.

She rolls her eyes at me, and I start to get nervous. I don't want them to think I'm a bad dad.

The doorbell rings, and Jules opens the door with a giant grin. I look at Jess again. She is glowing and radiant, but seems very nervous.

Sarah and their dad stand in the doorway with guarded smiles, looking unsure as they come into view. Another man, I'm assuming her sister's boyfriend Ethan, stands with a wide grin, and is the first to reach out and shake my hand.

"Hey, I'm Ethan. Thanks for having us. Brave move, inviting the whole family," he says with a laugh.

"I'm Julian, great to meet you," I say.

We all exchange introductions and hellos as they enter.

Everyone gathers around in my living room. I pass out small glasses of wine to those who want it, and give Jules a juice box. I'm hoping conversation will start itself, and it does, but not the way I wanted it to.

"So, Julian," Jess's dad says. "You're Jess's boss right?"

"Dad," Jess warns.

I smile. "Technically, yes. I'm the owner of the store, but I've handed over most managerial responsibilities to Jess.

She's the lead, and hopefully, if we continue the way we have been, the store will be fifty-percent hers someday as my partner . . ." I explain.

I haven't said this out loud to Jess, but she doesn't look shocked. She just smiles at me, and everything feels right.

Sarah leans in. "So how long have you guys been not just boss and employee?" she questions.

Jess answers this time before I can. "I met Julian my first night in the city, before I even knew he was my boss. We hit it off and really liked each other. Once we found out he was my boss, we tried to keep things professional. A couple months ago though, we couldn't fight it anymore. I knew I loved him, and Jules. It just felt right."

She leaves out the fact that I pissed her off and kicked her out, but the way she explained it wasn't a lie. It was a cuter version of the truth.

Ethan laughs. "Sounds like some kind of meet-cute from a rom-com movie? Did you spill coffee on him Jess?"

Jules interjects, "No! But Jess ran her shopping cart into ours and my grandma gave her my dad's phone number."

Everyone bursts out into laughter, even her dad. I feel my shoulders drop a little. The tension and nerves melt away. Jules, bless her, is a tiny little miracle who makes everything better.

Chapter Thirty-Three

JESS

By THE TIME WE sit down for dinner, everyone has softened. No one is on defense anymore or interrogating. They are just getting to know Julian, which is all I wanted.

I knew they would love him as much as I do.

Jules says, "Thank you Dad for the tacos, and thank you Jess for the beautiful hair" as we start to eat.

I reach over and give her hand a little squeeze.

"Always happy to braid your hair, bug!" I boop her nose, before picking up my fork to begin eating.

Sarah sits across from me, and when I look up mid-bite, tears fill her eyes.

"Sarah, what's wrong?" I ask, concerned.

"Nothing, just . . . proud of you. You've changed a lot. In a good way," she says, before wiping her eyes and eating.

As plates empty and conversation loosens, Julian seems to be genuinely enjoying the flow of conversation. Ethan is easygoing, as always. Sarah's sarcasm has a rhythm to it tonight, and my dad, though quiet, seems to be watching us with less suspicion now.

"So," my dad says halfway through dinner, "you cook, you clean, and you even have manners. You're making the rest of us look really bad."

Julian laughs. "Only on special occasions. Most nights it's just peanut butter and jelly or mac and cheese around here."

"That's true!" Jules says with blunt honesty. "But Dad puts the mac and cheese into the fancy bowls whenever Jess is here."

I blush, and giggle. "I didn't know there were different bowls."

"Oh yeah, we just use plastic ones when you're not around," Jules explains.

Everyone bursts into laughter again.

"Is that true?" I whisper to Julian.

"I guess it is." Julian chuckles, a small blush creeping along his cheeks.

For dessert Julian and Jules make brownies and serve it with plain vanilla ice cream. I hadn't realized how intimate it feels to share homemade food with my entire family. Every bite feels like it shows me more of who Julian is.

And I love every bite.

Sarah sits back, putting her spoon down, and wiping her mouth before saying, "So, what's it like dating with a kid? I can barely keep Trixie, my cat, alive."

Julian smiles. "It's . . . different. You stop pretending to be cool. You realize bedtime stories are more romantic than bars."

I reach for Julian's hand under the table, and give it a small touch of support. I glance over and my dad noticed. His gaze softens, just a fraction.

"You lost your wife a few years back, right?" he asks quietly.

Julian nods. "Five years. Jules was only one then. We've managed okay, but—" He looks at his daughter, who was currently licking ice cream off her spoon and humming to herself. "—it's nice not feeling like we're on our own anymore."

There is a minute of silence, but it's not uncomfortable this time. My family exchanges looks, something wordless passing among them, a collective realization that the situation hits close to home.

Jules breaks the silence. "I made a picture for everyone!"

She hops down, runs to the counter, and comes back with a crayon drawing of six stick figures around a bright yellow table, all holding hands. Above it, in shaky letters, she's written *Our Family Dinner*.

My dad stares at the picture a long minute before smiling and saying, "Really? That's us?"

"Yep!" Jules says proudly. "You're the one with the gray hair."

He chuckles, shaking his head. "Fair enough."

Later, after Sarah made us try her new coffee and we have another round of dessert "for Jules," the conversation turned to lighter things. Julian and my dad bond over football and old cars; Sarah and Ethan start teaching Jules a simple card game, which somehow turns into wild giggles and a cheating accusation.

After a while I lean in close to Julian and whisper, "They like you."

He looks over at my dad, who burst into laughter at something Ethan said. "Do they?"

"They're trying not to," I say, with a smile. "That's how I can tell."

A few minutes later, my dad raises his glass, with just water this time. "I wasn't sure what to expect tonight. But ... it's clear you two make each other better. And that's all a dad wants to see. Julian, you seem to bring out something real in her. So thank you for dinner, and for taking good care of my little girl."

I blink hard, as something in my chest tightens. "That means a lot Dad, thank you."

When coats are gathered, and shoes are being put on by the door, Jules tries to stall them with every trick she knows. One more hug, one more cookie, and one more look at her drawing.

Outside, the porch light glows gold against the dark night. My dad shakes Julian's hand firmly before leaving. "You've got a good thing here," he says to us quietly. "Don't mess it up."

"I won't," Julian says.

Sarah lingers behind after my dad and Ethan step down the walkway. Jules has gone to brush her teeth, and the house had the faint hum of after-company quiet.

"Well," Sarah says, "I like this, I won't lie. I was worried, ya know? I've been taking care of you since the day Mom passed. I was so nervous for you to move away, and for you to finally be on your own. I didn't know how you would do without someone looking out for you. I didn't think you could, if I'm being honest. But, you took a jackhammer to every expectation I had. When you told me you were dating your boss, a man with a child, it took everything in me not to completely lose it. I had to fight the urge to tell you that you aren't ready for that. That level of commitment, you can't take care of yourself, let alone a little girl. But I'm happy to say I was so wrong, Jess."

Her eyes brim with tears. "I'm not just proud of you. I'm in awe of you. I feel like maybe I held you back all these years babying you. But Jess, love looks so good on you."

Tears fall down my cheeks. "I love you, Sarah. You have always been the best sister, and friend, and you always will be."

I hug her goodbye, with the tightest squeeze, so I don't cry anymore.

"See you tomorrow, Jess?" she asks.

"Yeah, I'll see you tomorrow," I whisper.

"See you at the wedding Saturday, right Julian?" she shouts over my shoulder.

"Yeah! See you then, Sarah!" he shouts back.

After one more tight squeeze, I turn around.

Julian leans against the doorframe. I smile at him. "That went really well!"

He laughs. "And nobody interrogated me about my 401(k)s or our employee handbooks?"

"Not tonight." I chuckle. "But give them time."

He reaches for my hand. "I'll be ready."

From the hallway, Jules' voice echoes: "Jess, are you coming to read me a story?"

I smile at Julian. "Are you okay with that?"

Julian nods. "Yeah. I think she already decided you're part of the family."

Chapter Thirty-Four

JULIAN

As Jess disappears down the hall, I watch the candle-light flicker against the dishes that are still waiting to be cleaned. The night had been messy, imperfect, and exactly what I didn't realize I wanted. A table full of laughter, full of life again.

I blow out the candle and follow the sound of Jules' giggles down the hall.

A couple days later it's Brooke's Wedding.

I can tell Jess is stressed that morning when I see her.

I give her shoulders a rub, and remind her it's going to be fine. We trained people to handle all the flowers. All she has to do is walk down the aisle, not trip, and have fun.

"What if they put the centerpieces out wrong?" she asks.

"It will be fine, I'll come check them before any guests arrive," I tell her.

"You aren't even a florist!" she says irrationally.

"Yes, but I know what they are supposed to look like Jess. We went over it hundreds of times. It will all be okay." I try and rationalize.

"I feel crazy right now," she cries.

"You are crazy. You make me crazy. At the end of every day though, I realize I love your crazy. It's everything I've ever needed," I say while hugging her and rubbing her back.

She starts to cry. "I don't deserve you."

"Sure you do. Unless you are secretly hiding a whole other life as a serial killer that I'm unaware of." I laugh.

She giggles into my chest. "Nope, no secret life. Just this one."

"Then you deserve every good thing Jess. Relax, be happy. Enjoy today with your friends. Jules and I will see you on the wedding aisle," I say calmly.

"Okay. Thank you." She sniffs.

"Anytime."

I've spent the day getting ready with the groomsmen, and it's been fun but I miss my girls.

Jules is the flower girl today, because as it turns out Brooke and Lucas don't have a lot of kids in their life. Jules is over the moon about it. She says it's "been her dream."

Since the day I told her I'm guessing, because I don't think she knew what a flower girl was before that.

I tell the guys I'm going to go make sure Jules is ready to walk down the aisle. When I leave the room, the girls from the store are finishing up all the florals.

They look amazing. I know Jess was worried, but she trained them well. I go check in with my mom and Jules who are with all the bridesmaids.

Jules is so excited, twirling around in her dress. Jess turns around, and my breath catches. She is stunning. I mean, she always is, but she's radiating happiness, unlike earlier.

She looks confident, and has a glow to her.

She doesn't see me yet, so I just take in the view.

Jules whispers to me, "Isn't she the prettiest?"

"Oh, I don't know, I think she's tied for the prettiest," I reply.

"With who!" she shouts angrily. "No one is as pretty as Jess!"

"With you silly goose." I kiss her cheek. "You look beautiful, Jujubee!"

She smiles. "Oh, okay. I do look like a princess today."

"You look beautiful everyday," I say as I twirl her around.

Jess finally sees me and runs over. "How are the flowers?"

"Gorgeous, stunning, you killed it, and trained those girls well," I tell her.

"Really?" she asks.

"Really," I answer.

The wedding is flawless. At least from my point of view. We all have fun, and it's an unusual feeling to have so many people I care about in one place. We dance, laugh, and drink well into the night. Jess has her family and her best friend Lindsey with her. I have my mom, Jules, and my friends with me, and together we all come together and have the best time.

Toward the end of the night, David and I get some fresh air away from the wedding, and drink a beer together.

"Thanks, man," I say to David, holding my beer out to cheers.

"For what?" he asks.

"For getting me out all those months ago. I met Jess. It changed my life. I can't believe I'm sitting here happy like this today. With double the amount of people to care about and love," I say with a laugh.

"I'm happy for you man," he says softly.

"Yeah," I whisper.

"You know, Hannah would be happy too," David says, while staring at the ground. "Sorry, not sure if that was appropriate to say, but someone has to say it."

"No, I appreciate that. She would be," I say with a tear in my eye.

I blink it away quickly, because it's a happy night. "It's funny, I can almost feel her around us tonight. That sounds crazy, but Jules is growing up and is so much like her, and everything with Jess ... I was scared at first. But now, it feels like, well it feels like everything is going to be okay."

"Hey! Our song is on!" Jess shouts out the barn doors. "Come dance with me, handsome!" She winks, and heads back in.

"I don't like to dance, but I'd do anything to see that girl happy." I laugh.

David laughs too. "Yeah man, we all know."

And we head back inside, so I can dance with both my girls.

Epilogue

JESS

TEN MONTHS LATER . . .

"Good evening, everyone. For those of you who don't know me, I'm Sarah, Jess's big sister, and her built-in best friend since the day she was born.

"Standing here today, I feel a little like the proud gardener who's watched her favorite flower bloom. From the tiny bud who used to follow me around in Mom's heels, to the radiant woman standing here today, you've truly blossomed, Jess.

"Our mom used to say that Jess was her wildflower. Strong, beautiful, and perfectly capable of thriving anywhere. And I think she'd be so proud to see you now, finding the person who makes your soul grow.

"To Julian, thank you for loving my sister so deeply. You clearly *rose* to the occasion. And thank you for opening your heart to her, even after experiencing such loss. We honor and remember Hannah today too. Her love will always be part of the beautiful garden that's brought all of you together.

"And Jules, you are such a bright little sunflower. You've found another person who will love you endlessly, and I know my sister feels so lucky to be part of your world."

She pauses, blinking, and fighting back tears.

"I remember when we'd sit in the garden at the park with Mom, we would make flower crowns and talk about what our lives would be like. I wish she could be sitting in the front row today but I know she's here, in every petal, every laugh, and every tear of joy.

"Jess, you've always been my sunshine, and now you've found someone who helps you grow even brighter. You two are truly a *matcha made in heaven*. Okay, maybe that's more of a tea pun, but you get the idea.

"So here's to your love. May it keep growing, season after season, weather every storm, and always come back in full bloom.

"Let's raise our glasses to Jess and Julian! May your marriage be as timeless as a rose, as joyful as a sunflower, and as rooted in love as the family that surrounds you. Cheers!"

Julian and I sit at our wedding and look out at everyone we love. It was an amazing day. People were surprised we got engaged and planned a wedding within a year of dating, but we've lost a lot. We've lost parents, and Julian's lost a wife. When you know, you know, and we didn't want to wait any longer. We know better than most, that sometimes life has other plans.

During the bouquet toss, I try to purposely toss it at Lindsey, but obviously can't see exactly where I'm aiming. I throw it up in the air, and Carol does a crazy dive for it. I'm shocked she isn't injured when she jumps up in the air, bouquet in her hand.

Lindsey comes over cackling. "That was absolutely wild."

"I was trying to get it to you!" I chuckle.

"Oh, I still have plenty of time," she mumbles, embarrassed.

"I wouldn't be so sure . . ." I wink at her. She rolls her eyes, and we dance together for a minute, before I need a drink with my husband.

I head back to the table, where Julian is sitting, and sit down on his lap.

"Get a room!" Phyllis shouts.

"Close your eyes, Phyllis!" I shout before kissing Julian.

Phyllis was secretly bummed when I moved out of my studio apartment three months ago. She said it was because I was the cleanest tenant she's ever had, but I know it's just because she thought she'd miss me.

Luckily for her, she comes once a week for dinner now at our house.

I look out and watch Jules dance with Carol and Phyllis. I worry for a minute, because they aren't the best examples for that little girl, but they are just dancing. How much harm can they do in a four minute dance?

Carol and Phyllis immediately hit it off during the wedding festivities. I, of course, had them both at my bridal shower, and bachelorette party, and you would think they've been best friends for years.

Sarah's been mad at me for introducing them because Carol now calls Phyllis her "bestie for the restie." Sarah says she'll never forgive me for getting her replaced in Carol's life.

Sarah comes over. "How was my speech earlier?" she asks nervously.

"It was beautiful. You did amazing!" I tell her.

"I'm so happy for you," she says with eyes full of tears.

"Love you, Sarah," I whisper.

"Love you too," she replies.

I glance at the dance floor. All of my favorite people are dancing, and it makes my heart incredibly happy. Brooke dances with her husband Lucas, and over in the corner I see Taylor and Stephen dancing together.

Stephen is freaking smiling. It's the first time I've seen him smile. I nudge Julian hard. "Look! Stephen is smiling at our wedding!" I whisper-yell at him.

"I have a feeling we are not the reason Stephen is finally smiling." Julian chuckles.

I smile at Julian, just as the song changes.

"Can't Help Falling in Love" by Kina Grannis starts to play. Julian reaches over. "May I have this dance, wife?"

"Why, yes you can." I giggle.

We get up and move to the dance floor.

We dance a minute or so before Jules runs over and grabs my hand wanting to dance with us.

The three of us dance together.

"So what happens now?" Jules asks.

"What do you mean, bug?" I reply.

"What do we do with our lives?" she shouts dramatically.

Julian and I chuckle.

"I don't know. We never know what tomorrow will bring. But for today, we are just going to be a bunch of Flower People." I laugh.

Jules giggles. "Flower People! That's silly. I'm going to put that on my next bracelet!"

@glowkdesigns

Sneak Peek
BOOK PEOPLE

Ashley Claire

Chapter One

LINDSEY

IN THE SECOND GRADE I moved next door to Christopher Hemlock and my life has never been the same.

Christopher was my first love and he'll probably be my last.

We were voted "Most Likely to Live Happily Ever After" in high school, and while I guess we both lived happily, it certainly wasn't together like everyone imagined.

Christopher Hemlock became Chris Lock, an actor and international heartthrob. He walks red carpets with supermodels now, and goes to the Emmys every year. I think he's won four of them now, but I've tried to stop paying attention.

It takes a lot of effort to actually avoid news about Chris Lock. He's on every website, podcast, and magazine cover.

I live a happy life; books have always been everything to me. I found worlds to escape in, and fictional men to fall in love with. So when I inherited my grandmother's book store in Rose Point after she passed, it was practically a dream come true.

I'm comfortable. I love my job. I have great friends, and I really can't complain.

But the hopeless romantic in me, the one who reads every romance book before putting it on the shelf, wishes for someone to share this magical life with.

I can't find someone though, because there is this dark cloud hanging over every date I go on. A Christopher shaped cloud, one that keeps me from ever giving any relationship a real try.

Brooke's Wedding Day

The music begins playing. Soft strings, it's something classical and unbearably romantic as I start down the aisle.

It's ridiculous, really, how heavy a bouquet can feel when your heart's already carrying more than it should. The petals tremble slightly in my grip, betraying the nerves I've been trying to drown in champagne and smiles all morning.

And then I see him.

He's standing at the front beside the groom, tall and composed, hands clasped in front of him like he's not completely unraveling my entire sense of calm by just existing. The best man, of course he's the best man. He always has been.

I tell myself to look straight ahead. Focus on the altar, on the train trailing behind the bridesmaid in front of me, or on the hundreds of faces waiting to get the perfect photograph. But my eyes disobey, sliding toward him as if drawn by gravity.

He looks the same. No, worse, he looks better. His hair's a little shorter, the lines around his mouth a little deeper, the kind that come from smiling at a life that doesn't include me. And that smile, the half one, crooked on the left, hits me like a flash of sunlight I wasn't ready for.

I manage a small smile back, the polite kind, practiced and safe. The kind that hides more than it shows. My pulse, however, refuses to behave.

Step. Breathe. Smile.

It's all choreography, just like rehearsal, the rehearsal he conveniently couldn't be at. So I couldn't rehearse how to walk past the person I almost loved forever.

By the time I reach the front, I think he might say something. His lips part just slightly, but the music swells, and I turn to take my place beside the other bridesmaids.

I focus on my best friend instead, radiant and glowing as she steps into her forever. I'm proud of her. I am. But beneath that pride is that quiet ache, the one that hums along with the vows, reminding me that sometimes, love doesn't end dramatically. Sometimes it just stands across the aisle, looking perfect in a navy suit, pretending not to remember too.

The ceremony blurs.

Words float past me "love, cherish, forever" but they land somewhere far away. I keep my expression polite, my posture perfect, and my breathing measured. I listen to the photographer's clicks like a metronome. My best friend glows in lace and light, the groom looks at her like she's the only thing that ever made sense, and I try not to think about how once upon a time, someone looked at me that way too.

Him.

I can feel him at the edge of my vision. The way he shifts his weight, the low sound of his laugh during the vows, that small moment when our eyes accidentally meet and I forgot how to breathe.

By the time the ceremony ends and the applause rises like a wave, I'm exhausted from pretending. I follow the others out into the sunlight, smile for the photos, toast the couple, and laugh in all the right places. But when I can, I finally slip away to the quiet edge of the garden, under an old oak strung with fairy lights, and I let out a breath I didn't know I was holding.

And then, of course, he finds me.

"Some things never change," he says behind me. His voice is deeper now, a little rough around the edges, but still makes my heart race.

I turn. "You mean me hiding at parties?"

He smiles, and it's the same crooked one, though it carries something heavier now. "You always did hate crowds."

"I own a bookstore now," I say, as if that explains everything. "Solitude and quiet pays better than it used to."

He laughs quietly, the kind of laugh that makes me want to look away and never stop looking at the same time. "I heard. It's... impressive."

"I'm not famous," I tease before I can stop myself.

"Yeah, well," he says, scratching the back of his neck, a tell he's had since high school. "You wouldn't want to be. Trust me."

And that's when I remember the magazine covers, the paparazzi photos of his dates with super models, the face that fills and sells out theaters. The version of him that belongs to everyone now.

"How's the glamorous life treating you anyway?" I ask. It comes out lighter than I mean it to, but he hears the weight underneath.

He shrugs, and then looks down. "It's loud. Lonelier than it looks from the outside." Then his gaze lifts to mine, steady and searching. "Your shop ... it's in Rose Point, right? The one with the coffee place around the corner?"

I nod. "Rose Point Books."

"I walked past it once," he says. "Didn't go in."

"Why not?"

He hesitates, just long enough to make my chest ache. "Because I didn't know what I'd say if you were there."

The air between us shifts. The laughter from the reception drifts through the trees, muffled and far away. I can smell the champagne and lilacs, and something that feels like a distant memory.

I want to say a thousand things. That I missed him, that I stopped watching his movies because they hurt too much, that I still keep one of his old T-shirts in a drawer I never open. But all I manage is, "You could've just said hello."

He takes a step closer. "I'm saying it now."

The lights from the reception flicker through the branches, painting his face in gold and shadow. For a moment, the world goes still. It's just us, the oak tree, and everything we never said.

And then the music changes, and someone calls my name from the dance floor, and the spell breaks like glass.

"Go," he murmurs. "It's her night."

I nod, even though every part of me wants to stay.

As I walk away, I hear him exhale softly behind me, the kind of sound people make when they've been holding on too long.

And I think, maybe, this isn't the end. Maybe it's just the intermission.

Acknowledgements

First and foremost, I would like to thank my husband. You're my best friend and the only opinion I care about, so I hope you love this book as much as the last two. Thank you for listening to me rant about fictional characters I made up in my head. Thank you for loving me the way I hope everyone gets to be loved. I couldn't write romance without the absolute best inspiration, you! *XOXO*

To my kiddos, my little Peanut and Pickle—please always know your mom loves you more than anything. I'm so proud of you both and the people you are becoming. You can both do absolutely *anything* you put your mind to! And I'll always be here every single step of the way, to hold your hand (but only if you need it)!

For the readers, thank you. Truly, from the bottom of my heart. You'll never know my gratitude for you taking the time to read this book. It means the world to me. I always say I hope this is the worst book I ever write for you. I hope they only get better from here. And I mean it, I hope you enjoy every book a little more than the last!

To my parents, thank you for encouraging me to read and write throughout my life. Thank you for always telling me I could be anything I wanted. Thank you for buying my books and being proud of me, even though I know it's hard with the sex scenes. Your love and support mean the world.

Jenessa, my author bestie, neighbor, and life twin—I really couldn't do anything without you. I hit the jackpot when it comes to a best friend because you are truly the best. You make writing supportive female friendships easy, because you are the best example.

Chelsey—thank you for ALPHA reading the hell out of this book. Multiple times. Thank you for listening to me vent, rant, and complain. I'll forever be grateful. Your edits and commentary made me keep going when I second-guessed all my life choices. I don't think I would've made this book without you.

Book Besties, thank you for endless support and hype. Your encouragement keeps me going every time I want to quit. It's been the biggest upgrade in life to have the most supportive circle of friends around me. I cannot ever thank you enough for that incredible feeling. You all deserve every good thing, and I hope you all get everything you want in life.

Thank you to Sam Stringert, who I truly could not write a book without now. You're the best editor and I hope you know how truly appreciated you are!

Thank you to Athira, at @gloinkdesigns for working on ALL the art for this book and every book I've written so far. You make every character exactly the way I imagined them. I cannot thank you enough for your countless hours making all of my characters come to life.

Megan, @lemonlee.shop shall I compare thee to a summer's day? No, a summer's day is not a bitch. HEAR ME OUT... Thank you! Truly, from the bottom of my heart. I cannot tell you how much every support text meant. The nights watching DWTS on my couch with candy. I am forever grateful. Thank you for making the perfect discreet cover . . . AGAIN. And Thank you for putting up with every silly idea. You're the Schmidt to my Nick. Give you cookie, got you cookie.

To my BETA readers, Cassidy and Alexis, thank you for your support input and guidance.

Flower People

DRINKS

JESS' ICED TEA

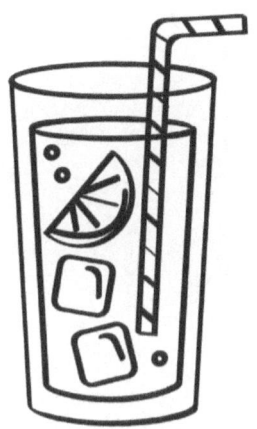

- 16 ounces of your favorite black tea, iced or hot.
- 1 ounce of honey syrup or honey
- Splash of Half and Half Cream

JULIAN'S BROWN SUGAR LATTE

- 2 shots of espresso or ½ cup of strongly brewed coffee.
- 1 cup of your preferred milk
- 2 tablespoons of Brown Sugar
- ½ teaspoon of vanilla extract
- Nutmeg and Cinnamon garnish on optional whipped cream

about the

AUTHOR

Ashley is a proud millennial Disney adult and unapologetic Swiftie, living her best life under the Arizona sun. A devoted mom to two incredible kids and happily married to her best friend, she's always found magic in stories—whether on the page, screen, or stage. A lifelong book lover, Ashley began her career as a high school teacher before transitioning into the world of editing and content writing. After years of helping shape others' words, she finally took the leap to chase her own dream: writing novels of her own. Now, she's all in! Creating sweethearts and swordfights one chapter at a time.

Follow along for updates on what Ashley has planned next!
Instagram: @ashleyclairebooks
Facebook: ashleyclairebooks
Website: www.ashleyclairebooks.com